"You've chan[ged...]
I remember."

Nathan thought he [...]
in Rachel's eyes w[...]
people change," he [told] her guardedly. "It comes
with living."

"That's one explanation."

Her continued scrutiny unsettled him, and he sat up.
"Maybe your memories aren't accurate."

"Maybe they're not." She sighed. "Perhaps I created
my own fantasy."

That was what worried him. He'd had only a year
with Rachel before he'd left for college. But during
that year, he'd learned more about her dreams than
most men could in a lifetime. He also knew her
fantasies.

"I'm not who you think I am, Rachel," he told her
gently. "I never have been."

She still insisted on seeing things in him that he
knew weren't there. From the beginning he'd
struggled with a deep dread that once Rachel
discovered the *real* Nathan Garner, she couldn't
possibly love him.

Dear Reader,

Hold on to your hats, because this month Special Edition has a lineup of romances that you won't soon forget!

We start off with an extraordinary story by #1 *New York Times* bestselling author Nora Roberts. *The Perfect Neighbor* is the eleventh installment of her popular THE MACGREGORS series and spotlights a brooding loner who becomes captivated by his vivacious neighbor.

And the fun is just beginning! *Dream Bride* by Susan Mallery launches her enchanting duet, BRIDES OF BRADLEY HOUSE, about a family legend which has two sisters dreaming about the men they are destined to marry. The first book in the series is also this month's THAT SPECIAL WOMAN! title. Look for the second story, *Dream Groom,* this May.

Next, Christine Rimmer returns with a tale about a single mom who develops a dangerous attraction to a former heartbreaker in *Husband in Training.*

Also don't miss the continuing saga of Sherryl Woods's popular AND BABY MAKES THREE: THE NEXT GENERATION. The latest book in the series, *The Cowboy and his Wayward Bride,* features a hardheaded rancher who will do just about anything to claim the feisty mother of his infant daughter! And Arlene James has written a stirring love story about a sweet young virgin who has every intention of tempting the ornery, much-older rancher down the wedding aisle in *Marrying an Older Man.*

Finally this month, *A Hero at Heart* by Ann Howard White features an emotional reunion romance between an honorable hero and the gentle beauty he's returned for.

I hope you enjoy this book, and each and every novel to come!

Sincerely,

Karen Taylor Richman
Senior Editor

Please address questions and book requests to:
Silhouette Reader Service
U.S.: 3010 Walden Ave., P.O. Box 1325, Buffalo, NY 14269
Canadian: P.O. Box 609, Fort Erie, Ont. L2A 5X3

ANN HOWARD WHITE

A HERO AT HEART

Silhouette®

SPECIAL EDITION®

Published by Silhouette Books

America's Publisher of Contemporary Romance

To Tara Gavin, for recognizing the potential;
To Debra Robertson, for making it happen;
And to Ed, for always.

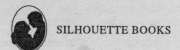 SILHOUETTE BOOKS

ISBN 0-373-24236-0

A HERO AT HEART

Copyright © 1999 by Ann Howard White

This edition published by arrangement with Harlequin Books S.A.

® and TM are trademarks of Harlequin Books S.A., used under license.
Trademarks indicated with ® are registered in the United States Patent
and Trademark Office, the Canadian Trade Marks Office and in other
countries.

Printed in U.S.A.

Books by Ann Howard White

Silhouette Special Edition

The Mother of His Child #948
Making Memories #1067
A Hero at Heart #1236

ANN HOWARD WHITE

discovered the romance genre straight out of three long, tedious years of law school—and instantly fell in love. She quickly became fast friends with a local bookseller who introduced her to the best the genre had to offer. Sandwiched between working with her physician/attorney husband and raising two daughters and a son, Ann read everything she could get her hands on.

She completed and sold her first book after becoming an active member of Georgia Romance Writers. She now writes full-time. The only downside, says Ann, is how much it cuts into her reading time.

Ann loves to hear from her readers. Please send your comments to P.O. Box 1539, Demorest, GA 30535.

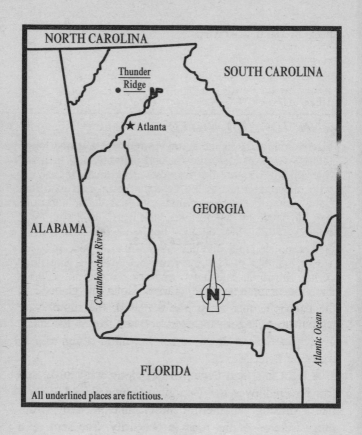

NORTH CAROLINA

SOUTH CAROLINA

Thunder
Ridge

★ Atlanta

ALABAMA

GEORGIA

Chattahoochee River

N

Atlantic Ocean

FLORIDA

All underlined places are fictitious.

Chapter One

For the umpteenth time, Rachel Holcomb glanced in the rearview mirror. As she'd feared, the motorcycle was still behind her. She tightened her grip on the steering wheel. Was it closer, or had her mind begun to play tricks on her?

A light mist had begun to fall along with dusk, and fog hovered over the Georgia mountains and valleys like a shifting, smothering shroud, unexpectedly wrapping stretches of the road in obscurity. She sent up a silent prayer of thanks that the possible winter storm had held off...so far. Around these parts, snow this late in March was indeed rare but not unheard of. As she cleared the latest blind stretch, her eyes again sought out the bike.

She forced her eyes back to the road and tried to dispel the frightening thoughts her imagination kept conjuring up. Had one of the bikers followed her from the hangout she'd just left?

The drag of the slowly deflating left front tire against the rack-and-pinion steering told her she was in trouble. Stupid! She understood the importance of checking her tires before leaving home, particularly in bad weather. The hazards of driving these mountain roads were well-known. Her only excuse was that when she'd left the house she'd been too preoccupied with worry over her brother Robert.

Or maybe someone had tampered with her tire at the last place she stopped? ''Get hold of yourself,'' she whispered and took firm control of her emotions.

The motorcycle had been trailing her since shortly after she'd turned onto the narrow, winding road leading back to Thunder Ridge. Sheer size indicated the biker had to be a man, she decided uneasily as she switched on the wipers to clear the increasing drizzle from her windshield. What woman was crazy enough to be out in weather like this? Well…on a motorcycle, anyway. Of course, the weather hadn't stopped *her*. But then she had a legitimate reason, she justified to the fates. She was trying to track down her brother.

Before twilight overtook them, Rachel had noticed the rider wore the traditional biker's uniform—dark leather jacket and skintight pants that hugged his massive frame. His black helmet gleamed ominously in the headlights of the all-too-infrequent oncoming traffic.

She'd met a few bikers around the area since she'd moved back to the small town where she'd spent her teenage years. Most were just ordinary folk who'd taken up motorcycle riding as an exciting but harmless form of recreation. But she'd heard rumors of others. The ones who kept to themselves. The ones who were up to no good. The ones she was afraid Robert was involved with.

An involuntary shiver shook her. She had no way of knowing which group the man behind her belonged to.

Well, she wouldn't stop until she had no other choice. Not as long as the motorcycle continued to trail her. She glanced in the rearview mirror again and exhaled a deep breath. The bike was nowhere to be seen.

But her relief was short-lived. Out of the corner of her eye she caught movement coming up on her left and glanced out the side window to see the alarming, faceless helmet of the biker, much too close beside her. Through the heavily tinted glass he held her gaze for the space of several frantic heartbeats. Finally he gestured toward her front tire, before dropping back to his former position several yards behind her.

Jerking her attention back to her driving, she concentrated on keeping the car on the road, while she uneasily analyzed her situation. She was at the point of riding a rim now. Trying to make it home on a flat tire wasn't smart, she conceded as she slowed to a crawl. These roads were tricky enough under the best conditions.

It would be a struggle, but she was capable of changing her own tire. Having lived in foster homes while growing up, she'd made learning how to look after herself top priority. Experience had taught her that asking for help usually came with a price.

The rain that had been threatening for the last hour suddenly began to fall in earnest. Of course, changing a tire in the dark on a rain-slick mountain road wasn't going to be easy—not to mention, safe.

Her choices were rapidly narrowing to only a couple. She could continue driving…and risk taking a shortcut down the side of the mountain. Or she could pull over to the almost nonexistent shoulder…and risk being hit by another car. Or coming face-to-face with the disturbing biker.

Well, she reasoned as she gingerly eased her right wheels onto the gravel shoulder of the road, staying alive at least gave her a fighting chance. She set the brakes, cut the engine, turned on her hazards…and prayed the bike would pass by.

But the motorcycle followed her off the road and pulled to a stop behind her car. In her side mirror, Rachel watched the stranger kick the bike stand into position, swing a long leather-clad leg over the machine and straighten to his full height. Oh dear, she thought. He was not only big, but much taller than she'd imagined. She sat absolutely still as he started toward her with an easy stride that seemed to say he knew he had all the time in the world. She swallowed and instinctively hit the master lock on the driver's door armrest. It gave a small courage-bolstering click.

When the man reached her window, he rested his right hand on the roof of the car and leaned down to peer inside. Rachel kept her eyes trained straight ahead. After several seconds, he tapped lightly on the tinted glass.

''Need some help?'' Even muffled through the double thickness of window and helmet, the masculine voice sounded rough…and sexy.

Sexy? Rachel stifled a rush of hysterical laughter at the absurd thought. Could someone contemplating a criminal act sound sexy? Stiffening her spine, she clamped down on her emotions before they got entirely out of hand.

Life had taught her to be realistic, to deal with trouble head-on. And realistically, just how much protection did a locked car afford her? If he was determined to get to her, the man standing outside her door looked as if he could make short work of any of her windows...and more. She switched on the ignition so she could lower the power window a scant couple of inches.

"I appreciate the offer." With effort, she kept her voice relatively composed. "But I can manage."

"Right, lady," he said with what Rachel decided was just a hint of exasperation. "And I'm impressed that you can. Believe me, under any other circumstances, I'd be more than happy to let you prove it. But not tonight."

"Why?" Did she sound as anxious to him as she did to herself?

"Why?" he repeated. "Maybe because you could get yourself killed?"

"I'll be fine," she hastened to assure him. "Really, you don't need to concern yourself."

"Yeah, well, tell that to my conscience."

She thought she caught just a touch of wry humor in the softly muttered remark. Or maybe she was indulging in wishful thinking. "How do I know I'm any safer with you?" Too late she remembered the tire iron she kept hidden under her seat for "safety" and mentally chastised herself for not retrieving it before the man had reached her car.

He straightened, looked in the direction of the tire, the rain-slick road and back to her. "You got a better choice?"

Probably not, she decided, searching for another alternative. The man was here, he'd offered to help, and cold logic told her to accept. Bottom line, whether she refused or not wouldn't stop him from hurting her if that were his intent.

His exasperation was fast turning into irritation. "Look," the man said, "just pop the trunk, and I'll handle the rest. You won't even have to get out of the car."

After another few seconds of deliberation, Rachel reached down and complied. Hearing the lock release, the man walked back to his bike. In her side mirror she watched him remove his jacket and helmet and stow them away, then turn on the bike's headlight and aim it toward the offending tire. He returned to the back of her car and, after a few minutes rummaging in the trunk, came around to her window again.

"Did you find everything you needed?" she asked. Her voice revealed the tiniest bit of strain.

"Everything except a tire iron."

Rachel felt herself flush. "Uh...sorry." She bent down, pulled the tool from under her seat and, without looking at her rescuer, pushed it through the small opening in the window.

"You know," he said conversationally, "a weapon won't do you much good if you hand it over to the bad guys."

Her gaze flew to the stranger. Without his helmet his features were illuminated in the motorcycle's headlight, giving Rachel her first clear look at his face. Her breath froze in her chest. Even after six years, even through tinted glass and the deepening dusk, she'd recognize him anywhere.

Nathan Garner.

He'd finally come home.

She steeled herself against the flood of emotions. When she'd decided to move back to Thunder Ridge, the possibility of running into Nathan Garner hadn't occurred to her. With his entire family gone, she'd thought there was no reason for him ever to return. Something squeezed painfully inside her chest. Of all the people who could have stopped to help her, why did it have to be him?

But there wasn't a flicker of recognition in his unreadable eyes—eyes she used to think contained understanding. Eyes she'd foolishly believed, a lifetime ago, could see into her heart and read her deepest dreams.

In slow increments, a greater fear replaced her earlier one. Nathan Garner presented a danger to her that went far beyond physical.

"Do you consider yourself one of the bad guys now?" she asked before she thought to stop herself.

As if he hadn't heard her, Nathan took the tire iron from her hand and moved to the front of the car.

Rachel sat perfectly still, trying to absorb the shock. She watched the back of his head and shoulders as he went about changing the tire. It took her several moments to get her heart rate steadied somewhere close to normal and to begin to think rationally. She knew how to take care of herself. She didn't need Nathan Garner to rescue her. In fact, the very last thing she wanted was to have to rely on him again.

She opened her door and started to get out. "I do know how to change a tire, so at least let me help."

"Stay in the car." He threw her a reproving glance over his shoulder. "How's it going to help if we're both wet?"

He spoke in the same deep compelling voice that had haunted her dreams. But now it sounded impersonal, as if he were speaking to just any casual acquaintance. "I can hold an umbrella," she said, pleased that she'd instilled the words with just a touch of disdain.

"Another light would be a heck of a lot more useful," he muttered, turning back to his task.

She should have thought of that. She retrieved a flashlight from the glove compartment, grabbed an umbrella from the back seat and climbed out of the car. Diverting the worst of the rain from his back, she directed the flashlight where she figured it would do the most good.

In spite of the rain and chilly spring air, Nathan had taken off his leather jacket. She couldn't help noticing how the soaked T-shirt fabric stretched to accommodate shoulders that had grown powerful during the years since she'd last seen him. His dripping hair, which she recalled as once being a shade somewhere between wheat and honey, appeared as dark as the approaching night. An odd little quiver darted through her midsection.

He wiped water from his face with the back of his forearm. "Can you hold the light steady, please?"

"Sorry." Rachel tightened her grip on the flashlight.

"Thanks." Nathan worked in silence for several more seconds. "I notice you still haven't learned to follow directions."

"So you *do* remember me," she said, determined to match his offhand manner. If he could pretend they'd been nothing more than casual acquaintances, so could she.

"I remember."

His words, terse and without inflection, produced a sharp shaft of pain that surprised Rachel. She'd worked so hard—been so certain—she'd long since put her feelings for this man to rest.

"You're right," she said, struggling to keep her tone light. "And I notice you still like to run the show."

Nathan made a grunting sound, and she wondered if it was in response to what she'd said or to the difficulty of what he was doing. "Shouldn't you be safe at home with your husband or boyfriend or...whatever?"

"I don't have a husband. If you'll recall, you didn't want the job." She allowed some of the churning emotions to spill over into her voice before reining them in. "I don't have a boyfriend, either. Or whatever." Unless, of course, Robert fit the last category.

Nathan stopped working and sent her a probing look, but his expression was unreadable. "Mind telling me why you'd want to go out alone on a night like this?"

His attitude was starting to rile her. "If it's any of your business," she said in a deliberately neutral tone, "I'm looking for my brother."

"Robert?"

"Yes." Though he'd never met Robert, Nathan had heard her talk about him often. That he remembered her brother generated an unwelcome softening within her. Careful, she warned herself. This was the man who'd promised her forever, then walked out of her life six years ago without a backward glance.

Studying her in the wavering light, Nathan stood, then rolled his shoulders as if easing the muscles there.

To give herself something to do, she held out the umbrella to him. "You're getting wet."

He shrugged it away. "So, you were finally able to get Robert out of foster care. He lives with you now?"

She nodded, still holding out the umbrella.

"I remember that was always a dream of yours." Nathan picked up a rag and began wiping his hands.

And do you remember the others? she wanted to ask. "At the moment, the dream part's debatable," she quipped instead. "This mothering business is a heck of a lot harder than I imagined."

"So I've heard." The first hint of a smile softened his face. "He's what, sixteen now?"

Nathan had always possessed an uncanny knack for remembering minute details about people. At least, about some people. He didn't seem to have lost that trait. "He likes to act as though he is, but he has a couple of months to go."

"Fifteen. It's a bewildering age," he commented, the humor in his voice deepening. "A daily struggle between the desire to become a man and the lingering antics of the boy."

"Well, I think antics may be too mild a term. And I think they're winning."

Nathan grinned, but it had a cynical edge to it. The Nathan she remembered had always had a quick smile—sometimes warm, sometimes cocky, sometimes heart-stoppingly sexy, but never cynical.

"Where's he supposed to be tonight?" he asked.

"Home." She released a breath. "Doing schoolwork."

Tossing the rag aside, Nathan began to gather up the tools. "It appears you haven't had much luck locating him."

"Not so far, anyway." It took Rachel a moment to realize that he'd finished changing the tire. Juggling the umbrella and flashlight, she picked up the tire iron. "I couldn't find him in any of his usual hangouts." At least, the ones she knew about. "He'll probably be home by the time I get there." She hoped. She prayed.

Separated from her brother when their last parent died, Rachel had fought long and hard to convince the court to grant her custody of Robert as soon as she'd established herself in her career as nurse-midwife. Yet she was finding that she was woefully unprepared for instant motherhood. There was so much she didn't know about the care and feeding of a teenage male.

Nathan set the flat in the trunk of her car, along with the rest of the tools, and closed the lid. He walked around to the driver's door. "I'll follow you home."

"There's no need," she said. "Thank you for changing my tire. I can take care of myself now."

He looked up at the night sky. The rain had slacked off, but giant snowflakes had begun to mix with the remaining drizzle. "You'll be driving on a doughnut in weather not fit for the devil himself."

"The roads are still clear," she noted, knowing that it wasn't cold enough to freeze.

"For the moment. But you know as well as I do, up here that can change in a heartbeat."

A memory flitted through her mind. She and Nathan stranded in a freak snowstorm. To keep warm, they'd huddled together in the front seat of Nathan's car, until their survival tactic had turned to something much hotter. It had been one of the few times Nathan's formidable self-control had slipped. But a patrol car had come along and rescued them—just in time.

She felt, rather than saw, his intent study, and she wondered if he was remembering, too. The need to put some distance between herself and this man came sharp and swift. He was awakening old memories and emotions she knew were best left undisturbed—memories and emotions she was certain he no longer shared, apparently had never shared. She shook away the thoughts.

"Look. You must be freezing. Why don't you go home and get out of those wet clothes?" she countered with less finesse than was her custom. She was used to soothing distraught husbands whose wives were in labor, for heaven's sake. Why was she having trouble dealing with one ordinary minister, someone she'd practically grown up with?

Her stream of consciousness skittered to a halt. *Ordinary?* Nope, she reflected wryly, wrong description. Nathan Garner had never been ordinary. He might no longer be the man she remembered, but not because he'd become ordinary in the intervening years.

"I've survived worse," he told her quietly, opening her car door. "Get in, Rachel. Don't make this more complicated than it has to be."

Rachel had heard that tone on too many occasions not to recognize what it meant. It was the tone he used when he wanted—no, *expected*—to get his way. He'd been very proficient at that when she'd been younger. Well, he was about to learn that she was no longer the naive, compliant girl she'd once been. That girl had ceased to exist the day she'd learned that her hero, the man she'd loved since she was thirteen, was a coward.

"There's nothing complicated about it," she told him, tossing the umbrella and tire iron into the car and sliding under the wheel. She deliberately made her smile amiable. "You do whatever you want. But I have another stop to make before I head home."

Chapter Two

He was no longer a Good Samaritan, Nathan reminded himself. Again. While keeping her taillights in view, he wondered what lunacy compelled him to trail after Rachel.

Maybe he could chalk it up to having had too little sleep since he'd come back to Thunder Ridge. He turned up the collar of his jacket against the cold air rushing at him. Hunching lower over the roar of his vintage Harley, he leaned into the next curve. It sure as hell couldn't be that it was a nice night for a ride or that he wasn't shivering in his damp clothes.

It seemed as if he'd been cold forever. He couldn't remember the last time he'd felt truly warm.

Locking away his feelings for Rachel the first time had been painful enough. He couldn't afford to risk opening them up again. But the urge to help warred with a hard-earned self-preservation that cautioned him that the only reward for helping her would be heartache.

He'd come back to his childhood hometown to settle his affairs here, then find someplace to exist quietly— and in anonymity. Someplace where he could find peace. He hadn't come back to awaken bittersweet memories of things he'd given up the right to years ago.

A couple of miles down the road, Rachel pulled into a packed-clay parking lot in front of a weathered building. The number of motorcycles parked outside proclaimed it to be a biker hangout. The garish neon lights screaming suggestive slogans announced that its reputation was at best questionable.

Keep going, he ordered himself. Rachel was a big girl now. She'd made it clear she could take care of herself. The bike vibrated with leashed power, as if assuring Nathan that it would deliver the speed necessary to escape the unwanted situation. All he had to do was turn the throttle and let 'er rip.

Yet he found himself again turning in after Rachel. He parked beside her car and briefly debated if letting her go in alone would expedite this little excursion. He was acquainted with the caliber of clientele that frequented a place like this. He knew what she'd find inside. Some biker hangouts were acceptable if not exactly respectable; he didn't have to confirm that this wasn't one of them. Still straddling his bike, he watched her get out of her car and, without sparing a glance in his direction, head for the entrance. The garish lights silhouetted her figure.

How was it possible that she'd become even more alluring than he remembered?

From the moment she'd come to live with his family at age thirteen, some instinct had told him that Rachel was different from the other foster children his parents had taken in. Unlike the others, his feelings for her had never been brotherly. There had been something about the solemn girl poised on the verge of womanhood that had gotten to him. She'd been skinny and scared, but there had also been an underlying defiance...and the promise of beauty.

And that promise had been fulfilled.

The last time he'd seen her, she'd been twenty-one, idealistic and full of plans, determined to take on the world. And with an iron will, he'd made certain he ignored how he felt about her...what he yearned for. What he couldn't have.

Now she moved with a self-assurance that was at once guileless and sexy. No, he couldn't let her go in by herself. Not dressed the way she was, wearing pants that seemed to follow her every curve and leather boots that could fuel a man's fantasies. Hell. He swung his leg over the back of the bike.

As she started up the rickety wooden steps to the entrance, he called to her. "Rachel, wait up."

Pausing, she turned and watched him walk toward her. "Are you still following me?" She spoke lightly, but with a hint of coolness.

Nathan smiled wryly. "What can I say? I feel responsible for you."

"Oh? I can't imagine why."

"Habit, I guess."

She stared at him for a heartbeat. "You broke that habit when you left Thunder Ridge for good after Matthew's death."

Her words hit him like a kick to the gut. It wasn't that he didn't deserve her scorn. It was just that he'd never experienced it before. "Some habits die hard."

"Look. Nathan." She folded her arms under her breasts, making him acutely conscious—even through her jacket—just how nicely she'd filled out. "I appreciate what you've done for me tonight, but I don't need looking after."

"No? Do you understand just how sleazy this place is?"

"I'm not here for the ambience. But you're welcome to leave any time. Robert's my brother, and I'm going to do whatever's necessary to protect him, even if it's from his own stupidity."

Again he felt the sting of her censure. Instinct told him to get on his bike and ride as fast and as far as it would take him. But he didn't. Six years ago he'd walked away. He was beginning to get an inkling that this time would be harder than he could possibly have anticipated.

"Then you shouldn't object," he told her quietly, "if I hang around."

Seeming to comprehend his logic as well as the futility of further argument, she pulled open the door and went inside.

Noisy, dark and filled with the rancid odors of smoke and liquor and perspiration, the place was jammed with people, mostly men. The few women present looked as tough as the men. An alarming number looked as though they'd rarely backed away from a fight. Catcalls and whistles, along with an occasional lewd comment, greeted her entrance, but Rachel refused to be intimidated.

Silently she agreed with Nathan. The place was sleazy. In fact, it was the worst biker hangout she'd visited during several weeks of trying to uncover where it was that Robert so frequently disappeared. She shuddered, imagining her fifteen-year-old brother in a place like this.

She resisted the urge to look back to see if Nathan had followed her inside, or taken her less-than-subtle hint and left. Her conscience pricked at her. No matter how she tried to convince herself that he deserved it, that *he* was the one who'd rejected her, deep down she knew she'd had no right to speak to him that way. He'd winced at her harsh accusation, and the memory of it left her feeling confused. Forcing herself to concentrate on why she was here, she began moving slowly through the crowd.

When she hadn't located Robert after several minutes, she walked up to the bar—little more than a wooden plank supported by a few barrels—and waited for the heavyset man behind the counter to notice her. She'd heard that this place sold liquor to anyone who had money, no matter their age. Now, having seen the place, she could believe it. Her concern for her brother, and the disaster he seemed intent on courting, increased to panic proportions.

The bartender ambled over to her. "Can I gitcha somethin', cutie?" he asked around the cigarette dangling from one side of his mouth.

She shook her head and held up a picture of Robert. "Have you seen this boy?" she shouted over the music pounding out of speakers suspended from the ceiling in all four corners of the room.

"Boy?" Without giving the picture a glance, he squinted at her through the haze of smoke in front of his face. "We don't serve no kids in here."

"How do you know?" she asked, waving the picture at him. "You haven't looked at this." A sentimental country ballad suddenly replaced the heavy metal beat of moments before. The sharp change in tempo and intensity left Rachel feeling as if everyone within earshot could now listen in on their conversation.

"Don't need to see no picture. Hey, Carl," he called to a tall, wiry man standing a few feet away, "you seen any kids around here?"

"Kids?" The man named Carl hesitated a beat. "Why?"

"This here lady's looking for one," the bartender told him.

The other man turned and ran his suspicious, intimidating gaze over Rachel. "None that I noticed."

Rachel had little opportunity to question the truthfulness of either man's assertion, or even to feel relief for that matter, before sensing someone standing much too close beside her. She looked up to find a bear of a man staring down at her.

"Hey, li'l lady, ya wanna dance?" he wheezed in her ear.

Her heart beat a nervous tattoo against her ribs. Again she caught herself wondering whether Nathan was somewhere in the room, and if so, how long it would take him to get to her should she scream. "Sorry," she told the man, keeping her tone polite, edging toward the door, "but I was just leaving."

The man's hand snaked out and grabbed her arm. "Betcha I can change your mind." The smell of stale beer on his breath was overpowering. "I dance real good."

"I'm sure you do." She tested her chances of escape against his beefy grip. It held fast.

"I'm real good adda lotta things," he slurred suggestively.

What had she gotten herself into? The muscles in her stomach tightened in apprehension, and this time she allowed herself to discreetly scan the crowd for Nathan's familiar face.

As if on cue he seemed to materialize from the smoky shadows. Rachel hated to admit it, but she'd never been so glad to see anyone in her life. He stood relaxed, arms loose at his sides, just out of her accoster's line of vision. With an almost imperceptible movement Nathan signaled her to keep silent.

Nathan was big, Rachel noted, but the man holding fast to her arm was bigger. He outweighed Nathan by a good thirty pounds of pure flab. And he looked mean.

"I don't think the lady's interested, friend," Nathan said, his voice level and low.

The man didn't bother to turn his head in Nathan's direction. "You don't sound like no friend of mine."

"Probably because you don't know me."

"Then butt out."

"'Fraid I can't do that. Not until you let the lady go."

"This here's between me 'n' her."

Nathan settled his questioning gaze briefly on Rachel. Rachel shook her head.

"The lady doesn't seem to agree."

The man spared Nathan a slicing look. "You the guy she come here with?"

"That's me." Nathan's voice still held a light tone, but he moved a step closer. "And I'd appreciate it if you'd let go of her arm."

"Think you can make me?" he asked with a sneer.

Ohmigod, Rachel thought frantically. All she'd meant to do was locate her brother. She hadn't intended to stir up trouble, or involve Nathan. And she definitely hadn't intended to provoke a fight. She hated violence. But something about the waiting stillness in Nathan's stance warned her to stay quiet and let him handle the situation.

He subtly shifted his weight. "The question is," he said, keeping the words pitched low enough that no one around them could overhear, "are you certain you want to find out?"

Maybe it was the intensity of his eyes and the quiet command in his voice that caused the other man to finally give Nathan his full attention. It had certainly gotten *hers*, Rachel thought in amazement. The air fairly hummed with tension.

As a girl, she'd known him to strike out to right a wrong, with no regard to consequences. But these had been spontaneous reactions, always motivated by compassion for the person being wronged. It had earned him the reputation of being something of a bad boy.

Now he demonstrated icy restraint. Somewhere along the line, Nathan had honed his skills. Now he displayed the subtle bearing of an accomplished fighter.

"Before you decide," Nathan continued, as if he were chatting with an old acquaintance, "you might want to consider a couple of things."

"Yeah? Like what?"

"Maybe you're good enough to wipe up the floor with me." Nathan held the bigger man's gaze unflinchingly. "But then again, maybe you're not. If that's the way it goes down, you're going to look pretty foolish in front of all your pals in here." He shrugged. "Either way, it's your call."

While his words sounded reasonable enough, Rachel shivered at the underlying steely edge. Not by a muscle twitch did he show a trace of fear. It was clear that he wasn't going to back away from this. This wasn't the Nathan she remembered, the understanding, compassionate man who had become a minister. What separated him from any of the others present in this room?

Rachel sensed something pass between the two men, some invisible sizing-up that only the male of the species seemed able to recognize and decode. She felt the hand imprisoning her arm loosen, then slide away.

"Whatcha got against dancing, anyhow?" the man groused, taking a step away from Rachel.

As if the subtle battle of wills had never occurred, Nathan grinned and gave the bigger man a friendly clap on the back. "It's against my religion," he told him cheerfully and began ushering Rachel toward the door. They left the man standing there with his mouth agape.

As Nathan hustled her through the door, she tried to add a bit of levity to relieve the tension, muttering, "Since when is dancing against your religion?"

But he didn't respond, just kept walking.

"How'd you do that?" she asked, once they were safely outside. "I've never seen anything like it."

A shadow of some strong emotion passed over his features, then was gone. "Just a survival technique I picked up here and there." He opened her car door.

She studied him in the dim light, wanting him to elaborate but not wanting to ask. "I guess I owe you one."

"Do you?" He flashed a Mel Gibson grin. "We'll have to discuss that some other time. It wouldn't be too smart to hang around here for long." He nodded toward the open car door. "Get in. I'll follow you."

"Really, you don't have to," Rachel told Nathan for the second time tonight, again sliding behind the wheel at his direction. "I realize it might not be obvious, considering everything that's happened this evening, but you're not responsible for me.''

''Just credit it to old times' sake.'' His smile turned wry. ''Besides, if you decide to take another little detour, I wouldn't want to miss the fireworks.''

She inserted her key into the ignition and looked up at him. She wasn't going to dissuade him. For whatever reason, he was determined to see her home.

Nathan Garner had changed. He wasn't the same man she'd known six years ago. Six years ago, he hadn't sent men bigger than himself running in the opposite direction simply by a look or a word.

Questions about what had caused the changes swirled through her mind. But speculating about him when he was this close, she warned herself, could lead to answers she might not want to hear.

She shook her head. ''I think I've had all the excitement I can handle for one night,'' she finally told him. ''Besides, you need a place to warm up, and like I said, I owe you.''

Behind the wheel of her car, Rachel concentrated on getting home safely. She glanced in the rearview mirror at the glare of Nathan's headlight behind her.

The house she'd rented for herself and Robert wasn't far, and the ride took only a few minutes. But by the time they'd pulled into the short driveway, Rachel had begun to wonder if she'd made a mistake by offering Nathan access to her home.

She stepped out of her car and walked to where he sat astride the rumbling bike. A solitary figure against the backdrop of darkness, he made no move to get off. The contrast between the man she'd once known and this remote stranger left her feeling oddly breathless.

Before, he'd been open, easy to read—at least for her. Now…

He looked lonely. As soon as the thought formed, she rejected it. She wouldn't allow herself to feel sympathy for him—she *wouldn't!*

She did not have time to waste on worrying about Nathan Garner. He'd made it clear years ago that he wasn't interested in what she could offer him. Her biggest concern now was Robert and how she was going to keep him from getting in any deeper with whatever it was he was involved in.

Even so, she felt compelled to ask, "Would you like to come in?" She had to raise her voice to be heard over the low growl of the bike's motor.

Once again the black helmet hid his expression. "Thanks, but I'd better go."

Briefly she considered accepting his refusal. She'd done what common courtesy demanded; she'd extended the invitation. Twice. But no matter how much her better judgment cautioned, she couldn't bring herself to so easily dismiss the man who'd come to her rescue—not just tonight, but on more occasions than she cared to think about in the past. He was cold and wet, and it was because of her—regardless of whether she'd asked for his help or not.

"Please," she found herself saying. "At least until you've had a chance to dry off and warm up."

"Ah, Rachel." He cut the engine, then removed his helmet and rested it against his thigh. "Still playing the little caretaker."

Without the helmet she was able to read the mild chastisement in his eyes but refused to respond to it. "No, Nathan," she said. "I'm merely returning a favor."

He became still, all teasing gone. "You don't have to repay me."

"I know," she said softly, almost wistfully.

So he wouldn't have to look at Rachel's expression, Nathan focused on the house. Memories he couldn't afford awaited him inside. He hadn't allowed himself to think about the Lucases' home or its former residents in years. Kyle Lucas had been his best friend. They'd had some good times together here. It had been his second home. Nathan had heard the family was gone now—either moved on or dead. Like so much else in his life.

He looked up at the night sky. A few stars had begun to reappear as the clouds moved out. And he silently asked a silent God if He cared.

He brought his gaze back to Rachel. Dwelling on the past didn't do any good. He was smart enough to know that too much had happened to recapture what he'd lost.

"I hadn't heard you'd moved into the old Lucas place."

"That makes us even. I hadn't heard you were back."

"I got in late last night. The town gossips probably haven't had a chance to spread the word." He was quiet for several moments. "How long have you been back?"

"About three months."

"So, how did you end up here?"

She shrugged. "Robert and I needed a place to live, and it was available." A light wind had begun to blow, and she pulled her jacket tighter around her. "Could we please get out of this weather?"

"Why not?" he muttered, more to himself than to her.

His purpose in Thunder Ridge was to take care of

unfinished business. And while he hadn't anticipated having to face this particular aspect of his past, it definitely fit the category. He got off the bike and followed her up the porch steps. Watching the smooth sway of Rachel's hips as she climbed the steps ahead of him, he realized he just might have made a strategic mistake.

She unlocked the front door and stepped inside, leaving him to follow. "Robert?" she immediately called out.

The answering silence implied no one was home. She hurried down the hall toward the kitchen, turning on lights as she went.

Nathan followed at a slower pace. How many years had it been since he'd last sat in this kitchen, drinking milk and eating a slice of Mrs. Lucas's homemade pie? He tried to ignore the emotions pulling at him. He'd given up any right to nostalgic yearnings a lifetime ago.

Rachel checked the answering machine, then quickly scanned a corkboard hanging on the wall above the phone. The collection of notes, photos and other assorted clutter suggested that the board was used for messages. But from the flicker of concern that clouded her face, Nathan knew she hadn't found what she was looking for.

She straightened her shoulders and faced him for the first time since they'd entered the house. It was late, and worry shadowed her expressive hazel eyes. "I'd hoped Robert would be home by now. Or at least have left a message." She rubbed her arms distractedly.

Without thinking, Nathan found himself saying, "I wouldn't worry too much." Then he cursed silently. This urge to make things right for Rachel was beginning to make him edgy.

"You wouldn't?" she asked, skeptical. "Why not?"

He thought of his last ministry in the inner city of the nation's capitol and the horror that some of the kids living there were forced to deal with daily. "It's amazing what kids his age can survive. He'll probably come through the door any time now."

The lines marring Rachel's forehead relaxed somewhat. "Thanks. Even if it's a lie, I needed to hear it." She smiled, a pale imitation of the ones he remembered. He'd missed her smile, he admitted silently, reluctantly. To short-circuit the direction those thoughts would take him, he shrugged out of his damp leather jacket.

"I'm sorry," she said. "Where are my manners? You need to get out of those wet clothes."

"Oh, I don't know," he said, attempting to ease the awkwardness between them. "A little while longer and I might get used to cold and clammy."

Her smile was tentative. "The bathroom's upstairs on your—"

"I remember," he told her quietly.

"Of course. You know this house as well as you knew your parents' home." She ran her hands down the sides of her jeans. It was an unconscious gesture, one Nathan had seen hundreds of times when she was a teenager. One he'd found inexplicably…sexy.

And still did.

Wrong direction, buddy. That's what got you into trouble before. "Towels?" he prompted.

"In the hall closet." She waited for him to precede her out of the room. "Do you need anything else?"

Yes, he wanted to say. *To see you smile the way I remember, once more.* The desire was disturbingly strong to voice some of the longings that kept roiling around inside him. But he figured at this late date she wouldn't be interested in hearing any of them. "A dry shirt," he said instead, "if you have one."

She ran her gaze over him quickly. "I'll see what I can dig up that might fit you." Another small smile came and went. "Feel free to use the shower to warm up. Would you like me to have hot tea or coffee waiting when you're finished?"

"Coffee," he said quickly. He couldn't seem to get away from memories. Hot tea with Rachel was one he didn't think he could handle. He'd walked down memory lane enough for one day.

Chapter Three

Rachel had just set the coffeepot on the stove to heat when she heard the rumble of another motorcycle in the yard. Robert! She hurried to the front room and peered out the window in time to see her brother climb off the back of a friend's bike. She breathed a sigh of relief, thankful that he was home, apparently safe and unharmed.

This time.

Robert was so dear to her, and she so wanted to make up for all the years they'd been separated. How was she going to make him understand just how worried she was by his actions and choice of friends?

As the motorcycle pulled away, she absently noted that she could distinguish the sound of this bike from Nathan's more powerful one. Robert paused long enough to check out the Harley before heading for the house.

"Hey, Rach," he called as he burst through the door with a flurry of unusual eagerness. "What's a Harley doing parked in our driveway?"

"Never mind that," she told him as anger came close on the heels of relief. Conscious of the shower still running, she figured Nathan would be occupied only a short while longer, giving her limited time to hash out a few things with Robert. "Who brought you home?"

The eager look that always accompanied anything having to do with motorcycles was immediately replaced by his typical bland expression. She couldn't be certain whether it was the reprimand in her tone that curbed his enthusiasm, or the fact that he realized his behavior was less than what he'd normally consider cool. Either way, she refused to feel guilty. One of her greatest concerns was that she had yet to meet any of these people he associated with.

He shifted from one foot to the other. "Uh, just one of the guys."

Somehow she'd known that would be his answer. One thing she'd learned during the three years Robert had been living with her was that he was averse to telling her much. She realized that part of the reason was because living in foster homes tended to make a child wary of sharing.

She sighed inwardly. "Do you know what time it is?"

"Guess I forgot. The guys got to…uh…talking," he said in that careless manner that always set her nerves on edge and raised her suspicions.

"Whose bike is it?" he asked, some of his former excitement sneaking back.

Motorcycles were something her brother couldn't act blasé about for long. She crossed her arms, determined not to let him sidetrack her. Robert had become very good at that. "This is a school night," she reminded him. "And you have homework." Knowing the argument that would follow, she refrained from mentioning that he was too young to be out this late, school night or not.

"Stop worrying," he told her. "I'll get it done. C'mon, Rach, tell me who the bike belongs to."

She judiciously ignored his demand. "It's nearly midnight. Exactly when did you plan to do it?"

"I don't have much," he grumbled. "It won't take that long."

"Robert, you agreed you'd spend more time on your studies," she reminded him, striving for a tone that was more coaxing than critical. "You can't do that if you're out half the night with your—" she searched for a more accurate term, then gave up "—friends."

"Aw, man." He rolled his eyes heavenward and shoved his hands into the pockets of his jeans.

Rachel sighed again. By his posture she could tell he was bracing for The Fight. It was the same battle they'd fought so many times in Atlanta, the one that had convinced her to give up her fledgling nurse-midwife practice there and move her brother and herself back to Thunder Ridge. But she hadn't left it behind. It had simply followed her. There was probably a lesson here somewhere, she thought wryly.

"I'll make you a deal," she said, deciding to try her hand at outmaneuvering him. "You tell me where you've been, then I'll consider discussing the motorcycle."

Robert looked startled, and for once Rachel could practically read his thoughts. This was a new approach. In the past she'd resorted to threats or guilt or demands, but never barter. She could almost see the adolescent wheels inside his head searching for a way to counter her. She knew all too well that he'd never willingly say anything that might be construed as snitching on a friend.

Hands still in his pockets, Robert shrugged. "We didn't go any place special. We were just hanging."

She heard the water shut off in the bathroom and knew she didn't have much time left. "I don't think you've fully grasped how this process works," she told him with constrained patience. "If you want information from me, you have to tell me something I don't already know."

Robert scowled, realizing he wasn't going to divert her. "Aw, Rach—"

Nathan picked that moment to saunter into the room. "Thanks for the use of the shower," he said.

Rachel vaguely registered that Robert stopped talking, the argument forgotten. She also registered that Nathan's hair was damp from his shower and that he'd pulled on his leather pants.

But it was his chest—his very *bare* chest—that grabbed her full attention. It reminded her, as little else could, that she hadn't been able to find a shirt that would come close to fitting him.

Finely honed muscles, rock-hard stomach, sunbronzed skin—this wasn't the body of a man who'd spent the past few years locked away in some church. Who was she kidding? His whole demeanor fairly screamed he hadn't been anywhere near a traditional church in a very long time.

There had been nothing mysterious about the Nathan she'd known as a teenager. Against her better judgment, she couldn't help wondering what had caused the changes in him.

Robert took in the appearance of their unexpected guest, and his scowl deepened. "Who the hell's this guy?"

Her brother's profanity snapped Rachel out of her daze. "Robert," she said warningly, "you know I don't approve of your cursing. This is Nathan Garner. He's an old…friend."

He didn't take his eyes off Nathan, nor did he wait for the rest of the introduction. "Yeah? Well how come I've never seen him before?"

Unruffled by her brother's rudeness, Nathan sent Robert an amiable smile. "Probably because I've been away a long time," he said before Rachel could answer for him. He walked over to the teenager and held out his right hand. "You must be Robert."

Obviously displeased that this man seemed to know who he was, Robert ignored the friendly overture and took a step away from him. Though several inches shorter than Nathan, her brother drew himself to his full height.

She remembered her own impression of Nathan the first time she'd seen him. Seventeen years old, he'd been dressed in jeans and a dirty T-shirt, and to her thirteen-year-old eyes he'd seemed a giant. But there had been an instant connection between them. Then he'd smiled his dazzling bad-boy smile and said, *Welcome to the family, beautiful.* And she'd fallen in love.

Somehow she doubted that was her brother's reaction. "You might be interested to know," she said, sensing a confrontation brewing and hoping to head it off, "that the bike parked out front belongs to Nathan."

Robert didn't look impressed. Gone was his interest

in the motorcycle. In its place was an overprotectiveness she didn't recall witnessing before in her brother. "You think you can just come in here," he said, gesturing at Nathan with youthful indignity bordering on belligerence, "and parade around in front of my sister like that?"

Still off balance by her own reaction to Nathan, Rachel almost didn't register her brother's uncharacteristic behavior. At the moment he was anything but cool. He was acting more than protective…maybe even the tiniest bit jealous. And definitely disapproving.

"I think you've said enough," she told him. This time her tone held a note of finality.

"Well, what's a half-naked biker doing in our house?"

Rachel caught herself before she laughed out loud. The incredulity in his voice would have been funny if he wasn't so obviously serious. Out of the corner of her eye she saw Nathan waiting expectantly for her answer. She pinned Robert with her best "mad mom" expression. "Let me see if I've got this straight. It's okay for *you* to stay out till all hours with your friends—who just happen to be bikers—but *I* can't invite one into my home?"

For a split second Robert looked chagrined, then rallied. "You haven't seen any of *my* friends in here looking like—" his eyes cut back to Nathan "—that."

"So far I haven't seen any of your friends in here period, regardless how they're dressed." That was another of her concerns—that her brother hadn't chosen to bring any of them home to meet her. "Nathan has a perfectly acceptable reason for the way he's dressed. He got wet while helping me fix a flat tire. I invited him here to dry off."

Robert glared at her. "You know how to change a tire." It was just short of an accusation.

"Yes, I do," she said calmly. "But that doesn't alter the fact that Nathan offered his help with this one."

She sensed the struggle between adolescent bravado and burgeoning maturity, which recently seemed to be in increasingly short supply. His sudden protectiveness was oddly endearing, but she couldn't allow it to excuse his rudeness. She mentally shook her head. What was she going to do about her brother?

"Maybe it would be best if you went upstairs and got started on that homework." The very softness of her tone suggested better than a shout that Robert would be wise to comply. "And when you've finished, get some sleep. Tomorrow's a school day."

For a moment Rachel was afraid he might continue to argue. But oddly enough he appeared grateful, even though the look he threw Nathan remained hostile. "When's he leaving?"

She folded her arms across her chest. "When he's ready."

Robert seemed to realize that he was locked in a losing battle, and it was probably in his best interest to withdraw and regroup. "Fine," he snapped as he headed for the stairs. "I'm outta here."

Once Robert's footsteps had faded down the upstairs hallway, Nathan spoke. "You handled that very smoothly."

Her pleasure at his remark unsettled Rachel. She hadn't liked Nathan witnessing the disagreement between her and Robert. She didn't want Nathan involved in her personal problems.

"Thanks, but I'm afraid the jury's still out on just how effective it was."

"With teens," Nathan said, "I've learned to take it one step at a time."

She brought her gaze back to him. And his bare chest. The realization that she was suddenly alone with him crowded in on her. A sensual memory, long suppressed, came unbidden to her mind. The smell of early September. The heat of the late afternoon sun. The sound of cool water rushing over its rocky bed. The feel, the taste of Nathan's lips on hers. Hot...sweet...forbidden. Nathan telling her that he was taking a missionary assignment in some out-of-the-way country halfway around the world. Her eighteen-year-old heart crumbling into small, painful pieces. She pushed the memory away.

"I..." She swallowed, searching for something intelligent to say. She wasn't usually tongue-tied. But then again, it had been a while since she'd been confronted by something as blatantly...sexy as a near-naked Nathan Garner. "I couldn't find anything that would fit you," she said, trying to ignore his chest and finding it amazingly difficult. "If you'll give me your shirt, I'll throw it in the dryer."

He studied her for several heartbeats with what she was certain was just a hint of amusement, then went to retrieve his shirt. When he returned, he had a towel draped around his neck. It covered a good portion of his chest. Absurdly, she couldn't decide whether to be grateful, or disappointed.

"I'll meet you in the kitchen," she told him. Snatching the damp shirt from his hand, she hurried down the hall to the laundry room.

It took Rachel only a few seconds to shove Nathan's shirt into the dryer, set the controls and head back to the kitchen. Not that she was in any hurry to resume a discussion with the man she knew was waiting for her.

How long could she maintain her composure while talking to Nathan Garner as if he'd been gone only a few weeks instead of several years?

He was far sexier, far more intense than the man she remembered. There had always been something untamed about him. But she'd understood him…or thought she had. Now he appeared darker and seemed to be hiding secrets—secrets she told herself firmly she had no desire to uncover.

She would be wise, she warned herself, to remember that this was the man who'd asked her to marry him, then deserted her.

Nathan glanced up as Rachel entered the kitchen. She looked slightly shell-shocked. He sympathized. Robert was at an age that made him hard to handle, particularly for a woman raising him alone. But Nathan suspected her frustration was due to more than just the disagreement with her brother.

"Your shirt shouldn't take long to dry," Rachel said, smiling brightly. "Then you can be on your way."

"Are you eager to get rid of me?" he asked.

Momentary surprise crossed her delicate features. "No more eager than you are to leave."

His smile turned wry. "Right now what I'm interested in is something hot to drink. Hope you don't mind." He indicated the utensils he'd set out on the counter. "I made myself at home. It's another one of those habits," he said, recalling her earlier response to his remark about feeling responsible for her, "I can't seem to break."

He looked around the bright homey kitchen. He hadn't realized how much he'd missed a normal home life and its simple everyday rituals, like sitting around the kitchen table with family, talking and drinking something hot. Or maybe he'd learned to disregard his sterile existence. It wasn't that he'd had no friends in the years since he'd left Thunder Ridge. But his life had lacked the warmth reflected in Rachel's kitchen.

He wasn't sure he appreciated being reminded of what he'd missed.

The coffeepot signaled its readiness, and Rachel quickly busied herself with pouring the hot brew into two mugs. "Robert isn't usually this rude," she said, changing the subject, making it clear she didn't want to discuss old habits. She set a steaming mug in front of him. "But then lately, I'm never sure what to expect from him."

Nathan cradled the mug in his hands, absorbing the warmth. He'd let her skirt the subject for now, but he was beginning to get the inkling that sooner or later they'd both have to face the past.

"What he did tonight isn't hard to understand. He was protecting his sister."

Raising an eyebrow, she sat down at the small kitchen table in the chair opposite him. "Why would he think I needed protection?"

He chuckled. "One thing I've learned not to do is second-guess what goes on in a teenager's head."

"If most of his friends weren't bikers, *then* I might buy the idea of him trying to protect me from one." She shook her head and stirred cream into her coffee. "Anyway, I apologize on his behalf."

"No problem." He swallowed a mouthful of coffee. "Does he do this often?"

She gave a short laugh. "What? Argue with me about strange men in the house, or stay out till all hours?"

"Either." He studied her over the rim of his mug,

gauging the sudden glint of amusement that enhanced the green in her hazel eyes. He hoped it indicated she was beginning to relax. "Both."

She shifted, then sipped the hot brew, taking great care not to burn herself. "We haven't been back long enough for me to meet many men, strange or otherwise," she said, answering without telling him anything. "Robert's behavior is relatively new."

It appeared he wasn't going to have any better luck getting her to discuss her dating habits. *Well, Reverend Garner, you must be losing your touch.* He felt a moment's irrational disappointment and something else he knew instinctively was best not to pursue. He didn't have the right.

"Funny, I don't remember your being chicken," he said, lacing the words with amusement he didn't feel. It might appear they were having a friendly chat, but she was making it clear that discussing anything too personal was out of the question.

"Chicken? In what way?"

"You keep dodging the issue."

"Do I? Considering how long it's been since you've seen me, there are probably several things you don't remember about me." There was a forced lightness in her voice as she determinedly held his gaze.

"I wouldn't bet on it." He could tell her he remembered far more than was healthy for his peace of mind. That he'd tried unsuccessfully for years to erase her from his memory. But he wouldn't.

"All right," he said, conceding defeat. "Tell me about Robert. Where does he like to hang out?"

She hesitated, and he suspected she didn't like the discussion going in this direction any better. "Anywhere he can find a motorcycle." She set down her mug and sighed. "I'm probably overreacting. It's just that he seldom tells me where he's going. And since we moved up here, I haven't met any of his friends."

Nathan studied his mug. "You must know that's not unusual for kids today."

"So I've been told, but that doesn't make it less worrisome."

"Has he always been reluctant to have you meet his friends?"

She shook her head. "Before he got on this bike kick, I knew most of them—or at least I think I did. Then he stopped bringing anyone home. It's one of the reasons I decided to move away from Atlanta." She blew out a frustrated breath. "I'd hoped he'd lose interest in motorcycles...and the people who ride them."

One side of Nathan's mouth tilted up. "Should I be insulted?"

"Sorry. I wasn't referring to you."

The word *necessarily* hung in the air. "Ah, Rachel, I believe you're hedging again."

"Perhaps you're right."

The soft flush staining her cheeks brought another rush of bittersweet memories. Her face had flushed just this way the first time he'd met her. She'd been thirteen and he'd been seventeen. Years later, he realized he'd probably fallen half in love with her at that moment.

"I'm not opposed to everyone who rides a motorcycle. It's just that Robert is at an age where he can be easily influenced by the wrong people."

He nodded, as if accepting her qualification.

"I guess I should look on the bright side," she continued. "At least I didn't actually find Robert in any of the places I went tonight. And no one said they'd ever seen him there before."

She looked so hopeful that he hated to burst her bubble. But she'd need all the accurate information she could get her hands on in order to help Robert. "They aren't going to say otherwise," he told her gently, "if they think a minor's involved."

A small frown pleated her forehead as she digested that. "Of course, you're right. Why didn't I think of that?"

"You would have figured it out sooner or later."

Silence fell between them, and he waited patiently. It was a cultivated trait, vital in his line of work. Sometimes he learned a great deal simply by listening.

After several moments had passed, she asked, "Are you home for good now?"

He took a sip of his now cold coffee. "This hasn't been my home for a long time."

"Only by your choice." The edge was back in her voice.

"Was it?"

"Oh, I don't know. Six years. You had to have made at least a few choices that kept you away all that time."

Studying her eyes, he searched for some hint of the understanding she'd once been so generous with. "I can't deny I made choices. But I can't say they were easy or that I was happy with them." He reached for her hand, wanting to convey how sorry he was for ever having caused her pain.

But she abruptly pushed away from the table and went to fetch the coffeepot. "Forgive me. I seem to be precariously close to prying." She refilled her mug with fresh coffee. He noticed that she didn't offer to do the same for him.

"Do you really want to know?" He hated the awkwardness between them. It hadn't been present six years ago. They'd been able to talk for hours about anything. He realized he had only himself to blame, but that didn't stop him from hating it.

"I can't imagine why you'd tell me now," she said, "since you didn't bother to mention six years ago that you were leaving. Permanently."

"I did what I had—"

The shrill sound of the phone interrupted. Though it stilled before the third ring, Rachel stared at the kitchen receiver, frowning slightly. After a moment, she brought her coffee back to the table and slid into her chair.

"So, what brings you back?"

"Unfinished business." He hesitated a beat. "I need to settle Mother's affairs. Do something with the house."

She nodded, and the anger died in her eyes to be replaced by quiet grief. "I never got the chance to tell you how sorry I was about your mother."

He didn't want to see Rachel's pain. He didn't want to feel concern or worry or empathy for her or anyone. "Yeah, so am I."

An ache that had never quite healed spread through his chest. His mother had died five months ago in late fall. He'd been surprised, yet a little relieved, that Rachel hadn't attended the funeral. He couldn't help wondering if it was because of what had happened between them the last time he'd seen her, at his father's funeral almost six years earlier.

"I still miss them," Rachel said, laying her hand on his bare arm.

He recognized her touch as nothing more than spontaneous sympathy, a gesture she would bestow on anyone who had lost a loved one. Still, it was pathetic how greedily he absorbed the feel of her fingers on his skin.

He covered her hand with his, almost afraid she'd jerk away. For a moment the awkwardness between them was forgotten, replaced by shared memories of a happier time. "You were close to them. It must have been rough on you, too."

"Yes." Tears glistened in her eyes. "It was worse than losing my own parents."

The sound of footsteps clattering down the stairs intruded, and Nathan was keenly aware of Rachel withdrawing her hand just before Robert barged into the room. That he was upset was evident.

"That was one of the guys on the phone," he said to Rachel without sparing a glance in Nathan's direction. "He told me he heard you were snooping around about me tonight."

"The weather was bad. I didn't know where you were, and I was concerned," Rachel said, collecting herself. "If that qualifies as snooping, then I'm guilty."

"You don't have a right to embarrass me in front of my friends!"

The memory of how reckless Rachel had been earlier that evening because of her worry over Robert kept replaying in Nathan's head. On one hand, he'd been impressed by her courage and determination; on the other, he'd been appalled by her lack of concern for her own safety. He resisted the urge to offer his opinion.

"I fervently hope none of the people I saw tonight are typical of who you call friends." Rachel stood and faced her brother. "Until you're of age, I have the right—not to mention the obligation," she said, her voice even, "to make certain you reach adulthood. Preferably in one functioning piece."

He gave a derisive snort. "Bull! You just can't stand to let me outta your sight."

Nathan leaned forward in his chair and rested his arms on the table, the movement drawing Robert's attention. "Do you realize," he asked Robert, "the danger you put your sister in tonight because she was worried about you?" He half expected Rachel to intercede, but instead she folded her arms and waited.

An uncomfortable look passed over Robert's features, then he turned his indignant fury on Nathan. "It's not my fault. If she hadn't been spying, she wouldn't have been in any danger. *She* did it because she's always sticking her nose in my business. I don't need anybody worrying about me. I'm old enough to take care of myself."

"I see," Nathan said reasonably. "No one needs to worry about you because you can take care of yourself."

"Yeah—" Robert shifted uncomfortably "—that's right."

"Okay," Nathan continued, acting as if he bought the argument. "So, why were you so concerned about your sister when you got home tonight? Isn't she old enough to take care of herself?"

Robert looked momentarily confused. "Hey, she's my sister. I come home, and she's here with some bad-ass dude I've never seen before."

Nathan nodded. "You were worried about her safety, right?"

"Well…yeah. What else d'ya expect?" Belligerence had returned to his voice.

"Don't you think it might be the same for her?"

It was as if Robert saw the trap closing, even before he was aware it was coming. "Hey, man, butt out. I don't want your nose in my business, either."

Well, thought Nathan, that line of reasoning certainly

wasn't working. "Tell me something," he said, trying a different tack. "What's so intriguing about biker hangouts?"

Robert seemed to examine this new approach for another possible trap. "Man, you can find some killer bikes around those places."

"You can find a load of trouble too."

Robert shrugged. "We don't go looking for it."

"You won't have to. Trust me, you keep hanging around places like that, sooner or later, it'll find you."

Robert looked as if he suddenly realized he might be entering treacherous territory. "That really your bike out front?"

Nathan nodded.

A spark of excitement darted across Robert's face, then disappeared. "Cool. I bet it's a dream to ride."

"Well, it depends on the weather," Nathan muttered sardonically. He was just beginning to feel that he wasn't kin to an Alaskan Polar bear.

"I guess it's too dark to take a look at it," Robert said, his longing barely concealed.

The fact that Robert had been concerned about his sister, even if it was on the primitive side, Nathan knew, was a good sign. It meant he wasn't too far gone. He hadn't walled off his emotions yet. However, Nathan wasn't certain whether Rachel understood enough about teenage males yet to fully appreciate this.

But the boy had an attitude. From long experience working with street kids, Nathan knew Robert was on the edge of making some bad decisions. He'd seen it too many times before. A little male guidance now might help push him in the right direction.

Whoa! What the hell was he thinking? He couldn't allow himself to be drawn into this situation. *You*

couldn't save your own brother; what makes you think
you can do any better with Rachel's?

He'd be smart to get out of there. Fast. "Maybe another time." Standing abruptly, he carried his mug to
the sink, trying not to allow the disappointment written
on Robert's face to play havoc with his conscience.
"Thanks for the hospitality," he said to Rachel.

"I'll get your shirt." She immediately headed for the
laundry room. Apparently she was as anxious to be rid
of him as he was to be gone.

So why did he feel so disappointed?

Chapter Four

Sunlight danced through the window of his childhood bedroom, nudging Nathan into wakefulness. It reminded him that he'd neglected to close the drapes before falling, exhausted, into bed late last night—or rather, very early this morning. He ran his hands over eyes gritty from lack of sleep. His gaze traveled around the familiar room that hadn't been his in more years than he cared to remember. Groaning, he thought of the day ahead, not certain he was ready to deal with it.

What he needed was a cold shower and a strong cup of coffee. Rolling out of bed, he headed down the hall to the bathroom. As he stripped off his shorts, a wry smile pulled at his mouth. He preferred sleeping in the buff. It gave him a sense of freedom, and it appealed to his sense of the absurd. There had to be something perverse about a minister who slept naked. But it was an indulgence he'd wisely abandoned. The last few years of working with inner-city street kids had taught him that being prepared was smarter than being comfortable.

He had a plan, he reminded himself as he stepped under the chilly spray of water, and for the sake of his own salvation he intended to stick to it. First order of business was to learn to keep his mouth shut. Last night was case in point. Whatever had possessed him to give unsolicited advice to Robert about his recent escapades was as baffling to Nathan as his uncontrollable urge to protect Rachel.

His plan was simple. Get the house ready to sell, take care of his parents' remaining business affairs, then search for a place remote enough that he might find a measure of peace. Seeing Rachel again had not been part of the bargain.

He'd believed her long gone from Thunder Ridge. His mother, in that quiet manner she'd a knack of using to convey her disapproval, had informed him when Rachel moved away shortly after he'd left for good. Then he'd deliberately lost track of her. Over the years his mother had kept him posted on news from his hometown, but they'd reached a tacit understanding that any discussion of Rachel was off-limits. He hadn't wanted reminders of what he'd given up.

Now she was back. He'd figured facing her again would be painful—only he hadn't anticipated just how painful.

He shut off the water and grabbed a towel. No matter how brief his stay, he knew he couldn't escape running into her. That was a fact of small-town life. What he didn't know was how many casual encounters with Rachel he could handle.

Take care of business, he told himself. Then leave.

If he didn't, he'd surely be lost. Rachel represented everything he'd turned his back on, everything he no longer had a right to think about, let alone yearn for.

But something told him that if he ever hoped to find peace, he'd have to deal with her. Rachel Holcomb wasn't the type to just go away.

Sorting through his parents' possessions and disposing of them held a somber finality. A part of Nathan hated to let go of the house and its furnishings. There was so much family history here. So much tradition. Yet he didn't think he could ever live here again with all the ghosts. Another part of him wished he could simply hire someone to clean it out, haul everything away and be done with it. But he wouldn't. This was his penance.

He glanced around his father's study. The last time he'd set foot in it was the day they'd buried his brother. It was a comfortable room, one that conveyed a sense of security and tranquility. It felt almost as if his father had just stepped away from his desk and would return momentarily.

But Nathan was all too aware that could never be, and he felt the ache—and guilt—as if it were only yesterday instead of years ago.

He walked over to the desk and ran his hand across its smooth oak surface. It stood in front of a huge picture window overlooking the garden and the mountains beyond. Sitting at this desk, his father had composed sermons, counseled church members, consoled grief-stricken families. And he'd done it with infinite patience and gentleness. Nathan had always believed he lacked those qualities—the very qualities necessary to be an effective traditional minister.

On one corner of the desk, his father's Bible lay within easy reach. Noticing the edge of something tucked between its pages, he opened the book and discovered an old photograph. It had been taken the day he'd announced his intention to enter the ministry. The entire family, including Rachel, had been present.

As far back as he could remember, he'd been an anomaly. His imposing size and forceful personality made him a misfit within his gentle family. His mother had done her best to teach him as she had Matthew to be a gentle man. But teaching gentleness to someone who towered over and outweighed most people wasn't an easy task.

Though his family had tried, he'd always felt an outsider in his own home. He suspected that was what first drew him to Rachel—they'd been kindred spirits. He'd sensed how out of place she'd felt as a foster child. With a wry smile he recalled that it hadn't taken him long to discover the more elemental reasons that attracted him to her.

He studied the snapshot. A good head taller than the others, he was flanked by his exuberant older brother Matthew and their beaming father. Their mother, small-boned and delicate, looked on proudly. Rachel stood slightly to one side, her smile as genuine, yet a little less enthusiastic. It was as if she'd somehow sensed that his decision would change their lives irrevocably.

He replaced the picture where he'd found it, between the pages of the family's history. His gaze was drawn to the line bearing Matthew's name. The first date marked his birth, the second his death. Nathan had witnessed his father's grief as he'd made that final entry. It was then that Nathan had realized he couldn't stay and witness it daily.

He'd failed his father, broken his heart, this man whose approval and respect Nathan had hungered for all his life. Though his father had never voiced an accusation, Nathan had read the silent questions in his eyes. His older son was dead, and it had been Nathan's responsibility to look after him.

The image of his brother's lifeless body still filled Nathan with anguish and impotent rage. He'd felt an overwhelming need to atone. But he'd never had the chance. His father had died suddenly, mere months later.

The last entry, in his mother's neat precise handwriting, recorded his father's death. Nathan closed the Bible, set it back on the desk and quietly left the room.

By the time Rachel arrived home, late afternoon was painting long shadows across the yard. Just inside the front door, she toed off both shoes and left them lying where they fell. She padded down the hall to the kitchen, thinking longingly of a quick nap. After a sleepless night and an early morning call from a patient in labor, she'd passed exhaustion several hours ago.

It was days like this that made her question her decision to become a nurse-midwife, especially while trying to raise her teenage brother. She relished helping bring new life into the world. What she didn't relish were the irregular hours that cut into her time with Robert.

The deep bass that thudded against the ceiling and jeopardized every light fixture in the house told Rachel her brother was in his room listening to what he called—with a perfectly straight face—music. She exhaled a breath of relief. At least tracking him down was one problem she wouldn't have to deal with tonight.

The kitchen, on the other hand, was a disaster area. From the looks of things, he'd done nothing to start supper. Nor had he bothered to clean up the mess he'd made fixing... She stared at the remnants of food smeared across the counter, trying to identify them, then decided that in this case ignorance was probably a blessing.

In her search for a dishrag, she encountered the empty mug Nathan had carried to the sink last night in his hurry to leave. She picked it up and absently stroked a finger over the rim. His restlessness, mixed with a raw hunger, had been palpable—though she doubted he'd admit to either. From their first meeting, she'd had this curious ability to sense things in him that he seemed determined to deny.

Suddenly conscious of the direction her thoughts were taking, she set the mug back on the counter with a sharp snap. Stay away from that trap, she warned herself. It held only pain. Nathan Garner's return to Thunder Ridge had nothing to do with her. Of that she had no doubt. All she had to do was stay out of his way until he'd finished his business here. With his family gone, there was no one left to keep him here or bring him back—certainly not her. He'd leave again, this time for good.

The familiar ache spread through her chest.

Hadn't she learned anything? She'd tried for six long years to forget him.

She'd failed.

Now she had to face the truth. If he'd had the power to crush her heart six years ago, now he could destroy her.

With all the windows of the four-by-four rolled down, Nathan smelled the promise of spring in the Saturday morning air. It had come early this year, making quick work of ousting winter's lingering effects. He thought of the bulbs he'd planted last fall in the rectory garden back in D.C. They'd just begun to send up shoots when he'd decided to return to Thunder Ridge, too soon to see the extent of their colorful display.

This was his third trip to the Salvation Army center with boxes filled with donations. He had others he'd eventually donate to the church. He'd made good progress the last ten days, he decided as he turned onto the old state road and headed toward his house. Still, there was plenty of work left to do. Maybe he would consider hiring someone to help him finish up.

Rounding a curve, he spotted a vaguely familiar figure several feet off the road, hunched over. Slowing, Nathan pulled onto the gravel shoulder and stopped. As he stepped out of the van, he recognized who it was. "Robert?" He walked over to where the teenager had dropped to his knees on the chilly ground.

"Go away," he said without glancing at Nathan. "Leave me alone."

There was a part of Nathan that would like nothing better, and he wondered longingly if there was a place without anyone around for miles who might need his help. But he couldn't drive away and leave the kid, anymore than he could have driven off and left Rachel that night a couple of weeks ago.

"Afraid I'm not that easy to get rid of," Nathan said, accepting the inevitable. "Are you okay?"

Holding his stomach and rocking back and forth, Robert looked up at him. His skin was a sickly shade of green. "Man, I feel awful."

Nathan hunkered down beside him. "What's

wrong?'' It was then that he picked up a strong whiff of alcohol.

''I think…'' Robert said between groans ''…I'm gonna be sick.''

He didn't doubt it; the kid smelled like an illegal still. Nathan placed a steadying hand on Robert's shoulder while he retched. ''Better now?''

Robert nodded weakly, and Nathan passed him a handkerchief. He took the cloth and wiped his face.

''What are you doing out here by yourself?'' Nathan asked.

''Friends…dropped me off.''

Nathan scanned the area. ''And left you? Some friends,'' he commented pointedly.

''Hey, man, don't dis my friends.'' His tone had become defensive. ''Whad'ya expect them to do?''

Typical of many teenagers, once the crisis eased, Robert resorted to belligerence to cover his embarrassment. ''Leaving you on the side of the road isn't an option I would've considered.'' Nathan patted him on the back. ''Come on. I'll take you home.''

''No!''

''No?''

''I can't go home.''

Nathan surveyed his now ashen face and frowned. ''Why not?''

''I don't want Rachel to see me like this.''

''You should've thought of that before you started drinking,'' Nathan commented dryly. ''How much have you had?''

The greenish cast to his skin reappeared. ''I don't exactly—'' he swallowed convulsively ''—remember.''

He didn't act drunk, and Nathan was beginning to suspect that more alcohol had gone down the front of his shirt than down his throat. He'd probably gotten sick after the first gulp or two. Which was a good sign; it indicated he wasn't accustomed to drinking.

While he felt a twinge of sympathy for the kid, Nathan also felt Robert deserved what he got for a fool stunt like this. Still, Nathan was almost tempted to smile. He'd learned in his own younger, somewhat wilder days, that the punishment that came with stupidity often was worse than the crime.

"Where'd you get the stuff?"

"I dunno," Robert hedged.

"Okay." Nathan had figured he wouldn't say much. Yet. "So what were you trying to prove?"

There was a long pause. "It was a dare. Y'know, we were…having a race to see who could drink the most."

All traces of sympathy left Nathan. "And do you think you won?" he asked softly.

Robert emptied the remaining contents of his stomach. "No." It was a toss-up whether he sounded dejected or irritated.

"Well, count your blessings. You could be dead."

"Huh?"

"Chugging alcohol can kill you." He stood up and offered Robert a helping hand. "I guess your friends didn't bother to tell you that part."

Robert began to turn green around the gills again.

Good, Nathan thought, at least that bit of information had scared him. Something he'd learned working with kids was that sometimes a healthy dose of fear could act as a great deterrent. "Get in the van," he told Robert.

"Where're we going?" His apprehension was clear even as he followed Nathan's order.

"To my place." He put the van in gear. "You need to clean up. And I can't very well leave you here."

Robert wisely chose not to argue. As soon as they arrived at the house, Nathan sent Robert to the bathroom. Twenty minutes later, looking considerably better, the boy reemerged and joined Nathan in the kitchen.

He motioned for Robert to take a seat at the table. "Drink this," Nathan said, setting a mug of tea in front of him.

He looked at the mug as if it might contain hemlock. "What is it?"

"Secret brew." Nathan wiggled his eyebrows in an evil villain parody. "Cures anything."

Robert took a sip to smother the smile that tried to break free.

"When you're finished, you need to let Rachel know you're okay."

A flash of alarm crossed his face before Robert concealed it. His mug hit the table with a thunk. "No!" he said. "You can't tell Rachel."

Nathan braced his hand against a cabinet and studied him. "Why not?"

Robert picked up his mug again and took a swallow. "Because she'll ground me for the rest of my life."

"I see." He walked to the table, pulled out a chair and straddled it. "Can't imagine why that might appeal to her."

Robert shrugged, striving for indifference. "Who knows? She gripes about everything I do." He eyed Nathan uneasily. "So, what're you going to do?"

"I haven't decided yet." Robert wasn't his problem, he tried to rationalize. He should simply take the boy home and be done with it. So, why didn't he? But he knew the answer.

He kept remembering Rachel, the way she'd acted when she'd first come to live with his family. At thirteen she'd shown the same defiance. It hadn't taken Nathan long, even at the age of seventeen, to understand that she used that defiance to protect a wounded heart.

The recent memory of Rachel's reckless determination to find her brother added to his concern. Maybe a few well-chosen words now would persuade Robert to discontinue his self-destructive course and keep Rachel from exposing herself to any more danger.

The glimmer of an idea began to form. "You like school?" he asked.

Robert squinted at him, clearly wondering where this was headed. "It's boring."

"Boring. I see. What kind of grades you make?"

"They're okay. Mostly Bs. A few Cs." Robert rolled his shoulders. "Of course, Rachel doesn't think so."

"Doesn't she?"

"Nah. She's always on my case about doing better."

Something else Nathan had learned while working with teens was to keep them off balance. If you kept them off balance long enough, they usually let something slip they hadn't intended.

"Pretty rough, huh," he said, sending him a sympathetic look, "asking you to do something you don't have the smarts for."

Robert bristled. "Hey, man, I didn't say that."

"Sorry. I must've misunderstood."

"Damn straight. I can do anything I wanna do."

"So you don't want to do well in school?"

"I didn't say that, either." He hesitated. "It's just that…the guys don't dig, y'know, nerds." As if suddenly realizing he'd said too much, Robert frowned. "Look, man, get off my case."

"Fair enough," Nathan said. He could afford to be amiable. He'd succeeded, if only briefly, in getting Robert to let down his guard. It was a start.

Confusion replaced Robert's belligerence. "Does that mean you won't tell Rachel what happened?"

"Not this time."

Surprise and relief replaced his confusion. "Hey, man, thanks."

"I'm not doing this for you," Nathan told him, his steady gaze challenging. "It's for your sister. She doesn't deserve any more problems. But if I ever catch you pulling another bonehead stunt like this," he continued, his words quiet but steely, "you'll answer to me. Understood?"

"Yeah, yeah," Robert said grudgingly, a new respect entering his tone. "Understood."

"I've got an offer for you," Nathan said, again changing directions.

"Like what?"

"I have a few odd jobs I need help with."

Suspicion played across Robert's face. "Doing what?"

"Cleaning out the basement and the garage. Loading boxes. Sprucing up the yard."

"That's your price for not snitching on me?" Robert demanded, his indignation clear.

Nathan chuckled. "Don't worry, you'll get paid, too."

"Yeah?" Robert brightened marginally. "How much?"

"A couple of bucks an hour to start. If you do a decent job, I'll give you a raise."

"Two dollars an hour? Man, that sucks!"

"That's my offer." Nathan shrugged. "Take it or leave it."

A scowl darkened his face, but Robert considered the offer. "Did you say garage?"

"That's right."

"Is that where you keep your bike?" Robert asked, suddenly taking a great deal of interest in what lay at the bottom of his mug.

"Uh-huh."

"Can I take a look at it, y'know, sometime?"

"It's out there. Don't see how you could miss it."

A gleam entered Robert's eyes. "Sure would be cool to ride it."

"Now *that* you'd have to run by your sister."

Robert grimaced as if realizing he might have pushed his luck a bit too soon. "Well could ya give me some pointers on, y'know, how it works and how to take care of it?"

Nathan had to work hard to keep a smile from ruining what he'd so carefully set up. "That might be arranged."

"Cool," Robert said. He shoved his mug around for a second or two longer. "I guess I'll take the job then."

"Good." Nathan stood and replaced the chair under the table. "Now it's time to call your sister."

"Aw, man, why? You said you wouldn't tell her."

"Two reasons. You need to let her know where you are. And you have to clear this job with her. If she says it's okay, tell her I'll drop you off at home in a couple of hours."

Robert debated a moment, then as if realizing it might be in his best interest not to argue, he went to the phone and dialed the number. A knock at the door prevented Nathan from eavesdropping. But as he walked down the hall to answer it, he could hear the murmur of Robert's voice.

Paul McDaniel stood outside on the wide front porch. He'd taken over as pastor of the local church after the death of Nathan's father. Remembering that the man could be very persistent when he wanted something, Nathan considered himself lucky to have evaded him this long. Exhaling in resignation, he opened the door.

"Reverend McDaniel." Nathan mustered a pleasant smile and held the door wide. "It's been a long time."

"That it has, my boy. Much too long." He stepped inside, grabbed Nathan's hand and pumped vigorously. "I'm delighted to see you finally came to your senses and moved back to Thunder Ridge. Your father would be pleased."

Paul McDaniel was in his late sixties and had always possessed an eternally optimistic outlook on life. Nathan didn't bother to try to convince him that he was mistaken about his father. "I'm here only until I can finish settling Mother's and Dad's affairs," Nathan told him. "Then I'll be leaving the area."

The older man's face fell. "But this is where you belong," he said. "It's your church. I've only been filling in until you returned and took over."

A noise from the hallway alerted Nathan that Robert had finished his call and come in search of him. Robert hesitated there, openly curious.

"Hello, Robert," the minister said. "It's good to see you. We've missed you at church recently."

Robert mumbled something unintelligible.

Reverend McDaniel turned back to Nathan. "I didn't realize you had a guest. I'll be on my way, then." He reached for the door handle. "But we'll talk again soon," he told Nathan, his good cheer restored for some reason. "So don't go thinking you've heard the last of this."

Nathan didn't doubt it for a moment as he closed the door behind the man. He turned to find Robert studying him with narrowed eyes.

"You're a *minister?*"

"Don't sound so horrified. The last I heard, it's still considered an acceptable occupation."

"I didn't think ministers blackmailed people."

"Some people," Nathan said, grinning, "need a little push. Did you talk to your sister?"

"She wasn't home." Robert shrugged. "I left her a message on the answering machine. Told her I was over here."

"Great," Nathan said, grinning wider, "that gives us time to get started on the garage."

As they headed out the back door, his good mood faltered. If Robert worked for him, Nathan was bound to have frequent contact with Rachel. But it would only be for a short time, he tried to reassure himself. He could handle that.

Couldn't he?

Chapter Five

It was almost six o'clock when Rachel drove up the Garner driveway. An orange-red sun hung low in the western sky, splashing crimson and amber and magenta and touches of navy across the landscape. Built on a large section of land some distance outside town, the old stone house perched on a hill that provided a spectacular view of the surrounding mountains.

From the first moment she'd spotted it from the front seat of a social worker's car fourteen years ago, she'd loved the place. Big and sprawling, it was perfect for kids—lots of them. And the Garners had generously shared it with many who were less fortunate. She'd missed it. She hadn't been back since the death of Nathan's mother several months ago.

At one time she'd foolishly believed that she and Nathan would eventually settle here, raise a family.... Determinedly she pushed aside those thoughts and stepped out of the car. For a few moments she allowed the serenity of the view to soothe the empty ache she'd been so sure, until recently, she'd put to rest. Taking a deep breath, she started toward the wide porch steps and the problems she knew waited inside.

When no one answered her knock, she went around to the back. A separate garage, large enough to accommodate a couple of cars and leave room for Nathan's motorcycle, sat several yards from the house. The smaller of its two doors was raised. Inside, Robert and Nathan hunched over the Harley, heads close together, deep in conversation.

She stopped a few feet away and studied them. What was it about motorcycles that her brother found so fascinating? To her, they were intimidating and noisy and potentially dangerous. And she'd learned to distrust many of the people who owned them. After several moments, curiosity drew her closer.

"If you're going to be a biker," Nathan was saying as he handed Robert something that looked like a wrench, "you have to know how to take care of your machine. Otherwise, you'll find yourself stranded in the middle of nowhere with shoe leather for transportation."

Her brother nodded, intently watching as Nathan showed him where to place the wrench and how much pressure to apply. Robert carefully followed the instructions.

Once he'd finished, Nathan clapped him on the shoulder. "Good job."

Robert looked at him and grinned. "What's a minister doing with a motorcycle anyway?"

As Nathan bent to gather the tools scattered on the floor, the play of muscles in his powerful shoulders drew her attention. "What can I tell you?" His voice sounded muffled, but she heard the amusement in it. "Not many people consider me your average minister."

Robert laughed and stooped to pick up the last few tools. "I can believe it."

The easy camaraderie between the two generated an ache deep inside her. This was the first time she'd seen Nathan relax since he'd been home. And how long had it been since she'd received a genuine smile from her brother? She couldn't suppress a niggle of envy that Nathan seemed able to relate to him, while she couldn't seem to get the knack of it. But it was the possible unhappiness Nathan could cause Robert that concerned her more. What if Robert began to depend on their friendship? When Nathan walked out of his life, what would that do to her brother?

Since he'd been a baby, his life had been a series of upheavals, being shunted from one foster home to another. Until she'd finally convinced the court to grant her guardianship. She'd been so certain that bringing their tiny family together again would be best for Robert and herself. But lately, she'd begun to wonder if she'd been right. There was so much she didn't understand about raising a boy.

As if she'd spoken aloud, Nathan glanced up and caught her in his penetrating blue gaze. He held her spellbound for a long moment, before he straightened and walked over to her. Dressed in well-worn jeans and a dark knit shirt, he appeared anything but ministerial. Breathtakingly sexy, and just a bit mysterious, his unwavering stare too easily breached her defenses. She took a steadying breath. She was far from ready to deal with Nathan Garner.

"Hi," she said, hoping that speaking first would give

her a small advantage. "When no one answered the door, I decided to check out the backyard."

"I'm sorry," he said. "We didn't hear you drive up." His voice held a vibrancy capable of soothing a frightened child or mesmerizing an entire congregation. Or seducing a woman. It wrapped around her, heating the core of her.

Robert chose that moment to wander up behind Nathan. "What's up, Rach?"

Relieved to have someone else to focus on, she no Robert's clothes were streaked with dust and what looked like grease. "I was about to ask you the same thing. What are you doing here?" she asked, keeping her tone light. "I thought you were supposed to be at the library with a classmate."

Robert shrugged. "Plans got changed."

"So, why didn't you let me know?" On some level she realized she was being unreasonable, but her apprehension increased each time she discovered Robert wasn't where he'd told her he would be.

Learning that he was with Nathan had not lessened that anxiety. Her objections to him were for entirely different reasons. She was concerned about Robert becoming too attached to Nathan. And the effect it would have on her brother when Nathan eventually walked out of their lives.

"I left you a message."

"Yes, and I appreciate that. But it would've been better if you'd asked me first," she said gently, "*before* changing your plans."

His expression turned sullen. "You said you'd be gone most of the day delivering some baby."

Guilt pricked at her. It was difficult to argue with his logic. Still…

"It's partly my fault," Nathan interjected quietly, easing the tension that stretched between her and Robert. "I ran into Robert on his way home." He glanced at Robert. "He needed a ride. And since I had some odd jobs around here, I asked if he'd be interested in helping me out."

Rachel stared, first at Nathan, then her brother. "And you agreed?"

Robert shifted uncomfortably. "Geez, Rach, it's no big deal."

"No big deal?" she repeated, unable to keep the amazement from her voice. "I can't get you to fix a decent meal when you're starving. Or pick up your room when we're one step away from being invaded by the health department." There had to be something wrong with this picture. Her gaze traveled to the motorcycle a few feet behind them. "What kind of job?"

"Just putting junk in some boxes and hauling them over to the Salvation Army. Okay?" He glanced at Nathan, then back to her. "I was going to tell you about it."

"Now that would be a welcome change," she said dryly.

"Robert, why don't you go inside and get cleaned up?" Nathan suggested. "Give your sister and me a few minutes to talk."

Robert didn't wait to be asked twice. He bolted for the house.

"You know," Rachel commented, watching Robert disappear inside, "if you were to sell that formula, you'd make a fortune."

"Formula?" he asked, his steady blue gaze generating an oddly restless feeling within her.

"Whatever it is you do to get a teenager to actually do some work."

A quick smile transformed his face, making him seem a little less world-weary. "Ah. That." Casually he slid his hands into the hip pockets of his jeans. "No formula. Just a matter of finding the right incentive."

"Oh? And what incentive works for Robert?"

"The chance to work on the bike."

"I see." That, she thought ruefully, would certainly do it. She folded her arms and walked a few paces away. "It was thoughtful of you to offer him a job."

"I can use the help." He cocked his head. "Like Robert said, it's no big deal."

"Whatever he might say, Robert thinks differently. Unfortunately, I know how my brother loves motorcycles."

Nathan's smile faded. "Are we going somewhere with this?"

She concentrated on the fading sunset and debated how best to proceed. She worried about her brother's fascination with bikes. More accurately, she feared the consequences of that fascination. She knew the crowd Robert ran with wasn't to be trusted. She suspected he'd ridden a bike alone a time or two, even though he wasn't old enough to have a license. Contemplating where all this could lead frightened her.

Finally turning to face Nathan, she met his gaze with her own. "I don't want you encouraging Robert's interest in motorcycles."

He studied her for a heartbeat. "Why? It's something he loves. It'll keep him busy—and maybe out of trouble."

"They're also dangerous."

"There are things far more dangerous," he countered in a reasonable tone.

She'd forgotten how good he was at arguing his point. "Perhaps, but that's not the point."

"Okay. What *is* the point?"

"I don't want—"

He took several steps toward her and stopped an arm's length away. "Say it, Rachel. You've never been reluctant to tell me what you thought."

But that was before she'd learned how little what she thought—or felt—meant to him. "You're right." She shoved her hands into the pockets of her hospital scrubs. "I don't want Robert involved with you."

For a good ten seconds, Nathan looked stunned. Then he gave a half laugh that contained little humor. "I didn't realize my reputation had slipped quite that badly. Or is that your opinion of me?"

Neither really troubled her, though she recalled how a couple of weeks ago he'd easily put a much larger man in his place. What did she know about the man Nathan was now? She hadn't seen him in years. He'd left Thunder Ridge a man of the cloth and returned a...what?

But that was the least of her concerns. Choosing her words carefully, she said, "It's not your reputation or my opinion of you."

"No? What then?"

"How long do you plan to stay in Thunder Ridge?"

"What does how long I'm going to be in town have to do with whether Robert does a few odd jobs for me?"

She did *not* want Nathan to come riding back into her life on a white charger, making her depend on him, trust him again. It would ultimately leave her open to more heartache, this time far worse than before. Now she was a full-grown woman, not a starry-eyed girl. She would *not* risk that betrayal again.

Nor would she expose Robert to a similar fate. She realized he was at a critical stage in his life. She knew it, yet didn't know how to handle it.

"What's he supposed to do when you leave again?" she asked.

A flicker of emotion turned his eyes a silvery blue. "Look, Rachel, it's not as if I'm planning to adopt him."

Anger, and something else she didn't want to examine too closely, flared to life. "Don't come back into my life—our lives—and think you can take over. Don't pretend you can fix everything." She sucked in a calming breath. "After Matthew's funeral, you told me to make a life without you," she said, her voice low and carefully controlled. "Well I have. It wasn't easy, but I did it. Don't you dare try to pretend you're my big brother." Her voice cracked. "I won't allow it—do you hear me?"

A painful moment of silence followed her outburst. "I can promise you, Rachel," Nathan said, his tone devoid of emotion, "I have *never* thought of you as a sister."

A giant fist squeezed her heart, but she was determined to finish what she'd started. "I don't want Robert to learn to count on you, then have to learn how to survive when you decide to walk away." Absently she hugged herself. "After today, stay away from him. I don't want you to hurt him the way you hurt me."

She saw a muscle work in his jaw before he concealed it with a slow, lazy smile. He raised both hands, palms out, almost beseechingly. "Whatever you want."

But it wasn't what she wanted. It was the way it had to be if she was to survive.

Robert stomped into the house behind his sister. She'd been acting weird ever since they'd left Nathan's house. "I don't see what's the big deal about working for Nathan," he grumbled.

Rachel slammed the front door with just a bit more force than necessary, which he knew wasn't a good sign. "Any spare time you have should be spent on your studies," she told him succinctly. "Not doing odd jobs for someone who probably won't be around a month from now."

He wasn't certain what that had to do with anything, but Rachel's dark mood warned him he'd be smart to back off. Thing was, his mood wasn't much better. His one chance to work on an honest-to-goodness vintage Harley was going down the tube if he didn't figure out a way to change his sister's mind. "Who says I can't do both?"

She tossed her purse and keys on the hall table. "Nobody has to, Robert." Hands on hips, she turned to face him. "Your actions do the talking for you. Everything in your life is more important than your schoolwork."

"Give me a couple of weeks, Rach," he said earnestly, ready to plead if he had to. "I can do both. I'll show you...."

She closed her eyes and held up a hand. "I don't want you working for Nathan Garner. The subject is closed." To emphasize the point, she turned and strode down the hall to the kitchen.

He chewed his bottom lip in frustration, wanting to follow her, to keep badgering her until she changed her mind. This wasn't like Rachel. She didn't usually get *this* bent outta shape. Unless he counted the other night when he'd come home and found Nathan here. She'd acted weird then, too. He slowly headed upstairs to his room, contemplating as he went.

It was probably just as well anyway, he tried to rationalize. He doubted the guys would consider it cool, hanging around a minister. But Robert had to admit that, for a minister, Nathan Garner knew some pretty impressive stuff about motorcycles. He owned a great bike, too. And even though he hadn't exactly said so, Robert bet he could talk Nathan into letting him ride it sometime. Of course, he'd have to convince Rachel first.

More than anything, he wanted his own bike. He was tired of being a passenger, of depending on someone else to give him a lift. A couple of times, one of the guys had let him ride by himself. It had given him a taste of what it was like to control all that power, choose where he wanted to go. It had been a killer. It had also been illegal, since he wasn't old enough for a license yet. But in a couple more months…

In his room, he flopped down on the bed. He'd find a way to be around motorcycles. If he couldn't work for Nathan, then he'd figure out how to get in good with the bikers again. He frowned. Not that it would be easy after the way he screwed up this morning. He stacked his hands behind his head and stared up at the ceiling. He'd think of something.

No matter what Rachel thought, the bikers were cool. And he wanted to belong to the group. They understood who he was, why he loved motorcycles. But the memory of how they'd dumped him this morning when he'd gotten sick kept nagging at him. He refused to dwell on it. All he had to do was convince them that he wasn't a wimp, that he was tough as the next guy, cool enough to be a member.

He grimaced, wondering what he'd have to do to redeem himself.

Her heart pounding, the first thing Rachel noticed as she hurried through the front doors of the small community hospital was its antiseptic smell. She'd never minded that smell. It was part of what defined her profession, like the green scrubs she wore into the delivery room. To her, it meant caring, healing, new life.

But not this evening. This evening the smell reminded her of pain and grief and death.

She went straight to the admitting-information desk, relieved to see Molly Olsen sitting behind the glass partition.

"Molly—" Rachel had to pause to catch her breath "—they told me Robert was brought into the emergency room. Is he all right?"

"I'm sure he's going to be fine, honey," Molly said soothingly. "But they're still checking him over."

"When can I see him?"

"As soon as Dr. Mosely finishes with him."

"You're sure he's okay?" Since returning to Thunder Ridge, Rachel had come to think of Molly as a friend. They both worked in the same small hospital. She wasn't known for mincing words. But even though Rachel knew the woman gave straight answers, right now she needed reassuring.

"Come on around," Molly said, gesturing toward a side door that led into the small glass-fronted room. "You can wait in here with me. I'll let them know where you are."

Grateful, Rachel followed her friend's suggestion.

"Tell me what happened," she said as soon as she was inside.

"Some sort of motorcycle accident."

Rachel dropped heavily onto a nearby chair, briefly closing her eyes. "I should've guessed."

"Now don't go borrowing trouble. I'm sure it sounds worse than it is. He was conscious when they brought him in, which, as you know, is a good sign. Here." She shoved a clipboard containing a sheaf of hospital forms into Rachel's hands. "Fill these out. It'll give you something to do while you wait."

Molly's matter-of-fact manner helped ease some of Rachel's tension, and she almost smiled as she began filling out forms. A few minutes later, Dr. Mosely stuck his head in the door.

"Rachel," the doctor said, "I'd like to talk to you when you're through here."

Rachel handed the clipboard to Molly and followed the emergency room physician into an empty office across the hall.

"Robert's going to be fine," he assured her, closing the door behind them and gesturing toward two chairs. "Have a seat."

She sat. "What happened?"

With a tired sigh, he settled into the chair opposite her. "Sheriff Rawlins brought him in about an hour ago. From what we could piece together, he went a couple of rounds with a motorcycle. But we're not sure."

"Oh, my God."

The doctor waved aside her alarm. "Sounds worse than it is. Robert's a lucky kid. He's going to be fine. Really. We just don't have a clear picture of what happened." He chuckled and shook his head. "Your brother's been pretty closemouthed about the whole thing.''

"That's Robert," she agreed, just barely holding her apprehension in check. ''But he wouldn't be in the hospital if he wasn't injured.''

"He sustained a pretty good whack on the head, but there's no sign of concussion. Says he wasn't knocked out. Has a nice assortment of bruises, though, and he needed a few sutures.''

She closed her eyes again and sent up a silent prayer of thanks. ''Nothing broken?''

"No. Young bones can withstand a lot of abuse.''

She didn't like the sound of that. ''Can I take him home?''

"We want to keep him overnight for observation.''

Her apprehension took an upward swing. ''Is that necessary?''

"Everything looks fine, but we want to play it safe.'' He reached over and patted her arm reassuringly. ''Come on,'' he said, standing. ''I'll take you up to see him.''

Entering her brother's hospital room, Rachel found him groggy and subdued, his lanky body appearing smaller in the white hospital bed. A rainbow of bruises marred his young face. A two-centimeter cut along his jaw had required about a dozen sutures; she hoped it wouldn't leave a scar. There was another uglier cut on his left forearm. His eyes fluttered open when she touched his hand.

"How're you doing?'' she asked softly, trying to keep the anxiety from her voice and her desire to shake sense into him under control.

"Okay, I guess.''

"Oh, Robert, what happened?"

He shrugged, grimacing at the movement. "It's no big deal."

She was beginning to hate that particular phrase. His closemouthed attitude and casual dismissal of his injuries almost got the better of her. Struggling to hold her anger in check, she reminded herself that he'd been injured and was in pain. Even so, she intended to learn what happened.

"Dr. Mosely said your injuries had something to do with a motorcycle?"

"What if it did?" he said, immediately becoming defensive.

So that much was true. "Whose bike?"

Robert looked away. "It wasn't Nathan's," he said, circumventing the question.

Fear mixed with frustration. Until today, Robert's problems could be considered more nuisances than anything else. Now he'd crossed the line, putting himself into physical danger.

"All right. If you won't tell me what happened," she said, losing the battle with anger and letting her concern for his safety take control, "then you leave me no choice. I forbid you to have anything more to do with these 'friends,' as you call them. I won't sit by and allow you to keep putting yourself in danger."

He rounded on her, even though the sudden movement obviously hurt. "First you won't let me work for Nathan—and he's a minister! Now you tell me to stay away from my friends. What are you going to want next? You just don't want me to have a life, do you?"

His outburst stunned her. Was she being unreasonable? Her brother was so dear to her. She knew his years away from her had been less than happy, going from one foster home to another. Now, she wanted only the best for him—to make up for those years. No, she thought adamantly, she was not being unreasonable. At least not regarding these nameless, faceless people Robert kept associating with.

But perhaps she had made a critical error in judgment by telling Robert to stay away from Nathan.

A movement caught her attention. She glanced up to find Nathan Garner standing in the doorway.

Chapter Six

God must be trying to tell him something, Nathan decided as he strode down the corridor. He hated the smell of a hospital. Having been in enough of them with his street kids and various members of their families, he'd long ago come to associate the smell with all the misery life could inflict on mankind.

He'd wanted to ignore Paul McDaniel's phone call telling him that Robert had been brought into the hospital. Nathan hadn't wanted to know that the kid was pretty banged up. Rachel had made it explicitly clear that he was to have nothing more to do with her brother. Or her, for that matter. Her last words to him still echoed in his mind, each one a tiny painful stab to his heart. *I don't want you to hurt him the way you hurt me.*

Yet he understood where the teenager was coming from, with his love of motorcycles, his longing to feel a part of something. And Nathan knew without doubt that no matter how hard Rachel tried to prevent it, Robert would find a way. And from the sound of it, not a satisfactory one.

He heard the voices before he reached Robert's room. As he walked through the door, his gaze immediately found Rachel. Eyes glittering with concern, face flushed with anger, she confronted Robert as a mother tiger might one of her errant cubs. Her auburn hair was pulled into a loose braid that hung halfway down her back. A few strands had escaped, softening the effect. She was alive and vibrant. And incredibly sexy.

When her gaze connected with his, the sensual impact took him by surprise. It was a gut-level response, one he thought he'd learned to control years ago.

"Is this a bad time?" he asked.

A half-dozen emotions chased across her features before she responded. "What are you doing here?"

"Isn't this what ministers do? Show up in times of trouble?"

She visibly collected herself. "Not always."

Deciding not to address that cryptic comment, he answered her first question instead. "Paul McDaniel was visiting another church member who's a patient here. He heard about Robert and gave me a call."

"I must thank him for his thoughtfulness," she said. Nathan wasn't entirely convinced of her sincerity. "So you're here in an official capacity."

"I'm here," he told her truthfully, "because a friend's in trouble." He remembered all too clearly the agony of being alone after Matthew's death. Of having to control his own grief while he dealt with a foreign country's interminable regulations, made arrangements to have the body shipped home. He wouldn't have left Rachel to face even a fraction of that ordeal.

She held his gaze for several moments, then seemed to relent. "Thank you."

He crossed the room to Robert's bed. "How's hospital life?"

"It sucks," Robert answered tersely.

Nathan noted that the teenager refused to look him in the eye. "That's why I make it a policy not to become a guest if I can help it."

Out of the corner of his eye, Nathan saw Rachel rub the back of her neck and knew the toll this situation had to be taking on her. "Why don't you take a break?" he suggested. "See if you can find a cup of coffee."

She hesitated, and he read the worry and exhaustion etched in her face. But he knew by her expression that the last thing she wanted was to leave Robert alone with him.

"Go on," he urged quietly. "How much damage can I do in a hospital?"

His comment didn't seem to ease her anxiety much, but she relented. "Can I bring you something?"

"No, thanks."

"Robert?"

Robert shook his head.

"Take your time," Nathan told her. "I'll look after him."

She nodded and slipped out the door.

Nathan waited until the sound of Rachel's footsteps had faded down the corridor before he spoke. "Seems you're determined to give your sister a rough time. You think she deserves it?"

"She keeps trying to run my life," Robert grumbled.

Nathan observed Robert's assorted cuts and bruises. "From the looks of it, maybe she should."

That comment met with stony silence.

"This is the second time you've been lucky. Doc says you're going to be fine."

"I guess," he said in a subdued voice.

"Want to talk about it?"

A look of feigned surprise crossed Robert's face. "Didn't Doc tell you?"

"I'm interested in hearing your version."

"I—" his eyes wavered, glanced away "—laid my bike down. Okay?"

"Your bike?"

Robert's face flushed. "One of the guys let me ride his."

"You know you're not supposed to take a bike out by yourself until you get your license."

"We weren't on the roads, okay?" he stated defensively. "We were riding out at the old Wilson place."

"Uh-huh. Let's cut to the chase. Don't forget, I've been around this block. You did more than lay a bike down."

"I don't know what you're talking about."

"Okay, we'll spell it out. You and I had an understanding, didn't we?"

Robert scowled, then nodded.

"That's better," Nathan said, his voice quiet but commanding. "Now, I want you to tell me what really happened."

Through the window of the hospital nursery Rachel studied the neat rows of bassinets and incubators. This was her favorite time of night. The lights were dim. The daytime hustle and bustle had given way to the quieter late-night routine. Most of the infants were asleep.

Tonight the scene brought back memories of the first time she'd seen Robert, the night he'd been born. She'd been eleven, and her father had been off somewhere "celebrating" the event. A thoughtful neighbor had brought her to the hospital to meet the newest member of the family. They'd gone straight to the nursery. Excitement had bubbled through her as the nurse wheeled Robert's bassinet over to the window so she could get a better look. Small, red and incredibly wrinkled, he'd captured her heart on sight.

But she hadn't gotten to visit their mother. She'd died from childbirth complications before Rachel ever had a chance to see her again.

Rachel had had one short year with her brother before their father had been killed in an auto accident caused by his drinking. Since they had no close relatives—at least, none willing to take on two young children—the court, in its bureaucratic wisdom, had separated them, placing Rachel in one foster home and Robert in another. It had taken her years to finally convince the court to reunite them. She'd been so certain it was the right thing to do, so hopeful for their future. But now… Again the doubts crowded in on her.

A nurse went over to one of the babies and picked it up. Spotting Rachel at the window, she smiled and waved. Rachel returned the greeting. She watched fondly as the nurse, a woman she'd met only recently, checked the baby's diaper, then carried the tiny squirming bundle to a nearby rocking chair to feed it.

It had never occurred to Rachel that one day her brother would be back in a hospital, this time with injuries from a motorcycle accident. It brought home again the fact that his problems went beyond what she was capable of handling. She was competent to help bring new life into the world, but it didn't appear she was competent to help her teenage brother.

She understood enough to recognize that he was searching for something—what, she wasn't sure. She'd been concerned that becoming involved with Nathan would cause her brother heartache.

Yet Nathan seemed to understand him. She'd sensed something pass between them earlier in Robert's hospital room. She hadn't been able to decipher it, but it reminded her of the sizing up she'd witnessed that night weeks ago in the biker hangout between Nathan and her accoster. Except this time she sensed it represented something positive.

It was becoming abundantly clear that she'd made a fundamental mistake forbidding Robert to work with Nathan. The benefits, she conceded, outweighed the liabilities. No matter how much her brother might come to count on him, Nathan could never hurt Robert the way the crowd he seemed intent on associating with had already proven it could.

But she knew it was more than her brother she was trying to protect. She was disturbingly aware of how vulnerable she still was to Nathan Garner.

At thirteen, she'd found it much too easy to fall in love with Nathan. He'd been daring, with a devilish sense of humor. But he'd had a gentle vulnerability she was certain few but she recognized beneath his bad-boy facade. When he thought no one saw, she'd watched him struggle with his decision to become a minister. She'd known it hadn't come easily. And she'd loved him all the more for it.

Until he'd broken her heart.

Now he was unexpectedly back in her life, a different man. There was an underlying gravity and sadness about him that had not been present before. It was as if he'd carefully tried to bury all his tender, caring qualities. Rather than the open man of her memories, he seemed to be hiding secrets. If he'd been irresistible before, he was devastating now.

Could she risk coming under his spell again?

She rubbed her arms, trying to ward off a chill. But none of that mattered. Her brother was in trouble. And to help him, she was beginning to realize she needed Nathan. He had the experience necessary to deal with someone with Robert's problems.

Robert was drawn to Nathan, seemed to like and respect him. Because of their common interest in motorcycles, Nathan had a way of communicating with her brother that she lacked. She couldn't compete with the crowd Robert was running with. And *she* certainly didn't own a motorcycle.

Nor could she ignore the fact that this latest episode came after she'd told him to stay away from Nathan. For Robert's sake, she'd deal with whatever was necessary, whether it be the devil—or a darker, more dangerous Nathan Garner.

She didn't have to become emotionally involved with him again. But even as she tried to convince herself, a tiny voice told her she was lying.

Would she be taking a serious risk pinning her hopes for Robert's salvation on Nathan? Everyone she'd ever relied on had failed her: her parents, the impersonal agency that had separated her from her brother initially. Even Nathan, whom she'd entrusted with her dreams and her happiness, whom she'd naively relied on to fulfill both. Until he'd broken off their engagement and left her with a broken heart.

Rachel caught the reflection of Nathan in the nursery window as he approached her. "How's Robert?" she asked without turning.

"He dozed off. Thought I'd better come check on his sister." He stopped beside her and casually slipped an arm around her shoulders.

She knew she should step away, but something more than the weight of his arm held her in place. The gesture was poignantly familiar to her, something he'd done countless times in the past. It had comforted then, and against her better judgment, she found comfort in it now. "You're very good at this," she said ruefully.

"You looked like you could use a little support," he said. "That or fall facedown on the floor."

"That bad, huh?" She tried to sound offended, but failed; his deep voice was too soothing. "Then this is an official rescue?"

He chuckled, and she felt the vibrations along the length of her side where it brushed against his. "Just trying to avoid having another patient to visit. I think I've reached my quota for this century."

Leaning away, she looked up at his face. "You sound as if you've had lots of experience."

His expression became shuttered. "More than I care to think about. The inner city can be a violent place."

She shivered at the bleakness she'd glimpsed in his eyes. A thousand questions darted through her mind, but she didn't voice them. She didn't want to know the answers. She might need his help, but she would not allow herself to be drawn into his life again.

He nodded toward the nursery. "Any of them yours?" he asked.

She smiled, not misunderstanding his question. One of them was indeed *her* baby, one she'd delivered yesterday. Experiencing a swell of love mixed with a deep sense of satisfaction, she pointed to a bassinet in a far corner of the nursery. "That one. A little boy. Well, not so little. He weighed almost ten pounds when he was born.''

He whistled silently and studied the unidentifiable bundle. "Do you like being a nurse-midwife?"

"Probably as much as you like being a minister."

He hesitated, and she sensed the sudden tautness in him. "That's not necessarily a good comparison," he said. "But I know what you mean."

Change the subject, her common sense urged. *You don't need to know about Nathan Garner's personal life.* "Did Robert tell you anything?" she asked.

A slight frown creased his forehead. "You know I won't…can't…discuss what's told to me in confidence."

She heard the gentle rebuke. "I wasn't suggesting… Well, maybe I was. It's just that I'm so worried about him." Her smile turned wry. "Okay then, I'll settle for a few words of wisdom."

Words of wisdom. That was the last thing Nathan felt qualified to give anyone—especially Rachel. It had been years since he'd felt anything close to wise. His source of inspiration had deserted him a long time ago. Still, he empathized with what she was going through. He understood all too well her concern for her brother. He'd been there.

He should tell Rachel good-night and get the hell out of there. But she felt too good nestled against his side, almost as if it hadn't been six long years since the last time he'd held her. And like a man denied sustenance too long, he greedily allowed himself this small pleasure.

"Afraid I'm fresh out," Nathan told her, keeping his tone light.

"Oh." The word contained discouragement. "I

thought that was a major part of a minister's job description.''

He debated before he spoke. ''The fact is, I'm not certain the title still fits.''

She pulled away to stare at him in shock. ''You mean you're no longer a minister?''

Reluctantly he allowed his arm to slide away from her shoulders. The separation added to his sense of loss. ''Let's say I'm giving that possibility serious thought.''

''But you can't.''

Her outright dismissal surprised him and made him feel oddly uncomfortable. He chuckled with little humor. ''Is there some law I'm unaware of that says once a minister, always a minister?''

''Yes,'' she said, studying him intently. ''I think for you there may be.''

''What makes you say that?''

''Because being a minister is a part of you. Always has been, always will be.'' Her gaze returned to the nursery window. ''But I'm certain you don't want to talk about it.''

''You always were perceptive.'' From their first meeting, she'd had an unsettling way of understanding him. Yet there were parts of him she'd refused to see.

''Yes, well, that doesn't seem to be the case with Robert,'' she said. ''It's scary. He's my brother and I'm responsible for him, but I can't figure him out. I don't understand what he wants or needs.''

He felt a niggle of guilt. No matter how he rationalized, she had a right to know what was going on with her brother. It wasn't as if Nathan would be betraying a confidence. Robert hadn't been that candid, but that hadn't prevented Nathan from reading between the lines. It didn't take much to figure it out. After his humiliating experience with the liquor, Robert felt he had to prove himself to the motorcycle crowd.

Trouble was, Nathan couldn't explain that to Rachel without revealing Robert's little secret. And Nathan *had* promised not to divulge that episode. But in return, Robert had promised not to cause his sister any more grief. It was Robert who'd broken their pact.

Rachel needed to know the danger Robert was placing himself in. Nathan understood what it was like to be responsible for a brother. Understood the frustration, desperation, terror of being unable to protect him. Understood all too well the anguish of failing.

"I won't reveal a confidence," he finally said, "but I can give you an opinion about what's going on."

"Thank you." Rachel placed her hand on his arm. "Believe me, I appreciate anything you can tell me."

"Robert's told everyone that his injuries came from laying his bike down."

"I'm not certain I know what that means."

"He lost control of it. His bike slipped out from under him."

She nodded, frowning slightly. "I see."

"But I think it had to be more than that."

"More?"

He hesitated. "Some of his injuries look more like they came from a fight."

"You mean, as in a fistfight?"

"At least."

Her frown deepened. "Are you suggesting that something more than fists were involved?"

"Very possibly."

She closed her eyes briefly, obviously not wanting to hear any more. "I had no idea it had gotten this bad.

He knows how I hate violence." She shook her head in frustration. "How can this happen?"

"What?"

"How can the very things I tried to leave behind in Atlanta have followed us to Thunder Ridge?"

"Violence, you mean?"

She nodded. "That was a major reason why I decided to move. I wanted to get Robert away from the stupid competition among young males determined to demonstrate who's the toughest by using brute force."

Nathan sighed. "Because it's not limited to any one area. You can't escape it. It's inside us. We have to learn to fight it on our own turf."

One side of her mouth turned up in a faint smile. "And you said you had no wisdom to offer." She rubbed her arms. "Robert should have talked to me about this."

"Maybe he didn't want to alarm you," he said. "Sometimes it's easier to talk man to man."

"Does it have to be that way? I'm the one who's supposed to take care of him, protect him."

Rachel saw pain shadow Nathan's face, and he remained quiet for several moments. "Sometimes no matter how much we try, we can't protect those we love."

Robert's problems, she now realized, were far more serious than she'd imagined, or was equipped to handle. This time he'd been lucky. Next time, he could be killed. "I owe you an apology," she said.

"For what?"

"I should never have told you to stay away from Robert. You're probably the one person who has a chance of reaching him before it's too late."

"No, you were right," he said. His voice had turned flat. "I have no right to interfere in your business."

She swallowed her pride and ignored all the warning signals buzzing in her head. "Even if I ask you to?"

His expression became remote, yet regretful. "I'm not the person you need. I'm not qualified to offer advice or to help lost souls. I won't even be here long enough to do Robert any good."

"I see." She moved a few steps away, determined not to let him see her disappointment or how his rejection hurt. "You're right, this isn't your worry. Robert's my responsibility. I'll figure out something."

He frowned. "Promise me you won't do anything foolish. Promise me you'll let Sheriff Rawlins handle it."

"Thanks, but don't concern yourself. I'll be fine. Really." She smiled brightly. "I better get back to Robert now."

She'd figure out a way to help Robert—with or without Nathan Garner, she thought as she watched him walk away. She'd learned to fight life's battles alone a long time ago. She wouldn't stand by and allow her brother to throw his life away.

Chapter Seven

"Hey, Reverend Garner, wait up a minute."

Damn, thought Nathan. He'd almost made it. He was within inches of the wide doors leading out of the hospital. And freedom. He raised his eyes heavenward.

It wasn't necessary to see the caller to identify him as Sheriff Harold Rawlins. The man had a drawl that was as distinctive as it was deceptive. He might sound laid-back, maybe even a bit hickish, but it was all a clever ruse. The man was a wizard at getting what he went after—whether a criminal or a favor.

"Evening, Sheriff," Nathan said and waited for the older man to catch up with him.

Harold Rawlins checked his watch. "More like morning, I'd say." He clasped Nathan's hand in a firm grip and clapped him on the back. "It's damned good to see you again, son."

"Good to see you, too, sir."

The sheriff chuckled. "Now that we've got the formalities outta the way, we can get down to business. You're a hard man to track down."

Nathan couldn't stop the grin. "Didn't think I'd been back long enough to give you reason to come looking for me…again." He'd known the sheriff as far back as he could remember, and on a number of occasions during Nathan's bad-boy years, Harold Rawlins had come looking for him—and with good cause. It had been the sheriff who'd pulled his butt out of more than one fire.

"Different reason this time," the sheriff said, chuckling again. "Wanted to get your take on what happened to the Holcomb boy."

"I understand you brought Robert to the emergency room," Nathan said.

"Yep. Damn spring vacations," Rawlins muttered. "Nothing for kids to do but get into trouble. Found him at that roadside park on the other side of town. Some pretty unsavory bikers hang out up there." He shook his head. "When I found the boy, he said he was okay, but he seemed a little rocky to me."

A sick feeling began to take root in Nathan's gut. "The doctor says he's going to be fine. He's damned lucky you came along when you did. In case no one's said it, thank you."

Rawlins waved away his gratitude. "He tell you anything?"

Again, Nathan was torn between revealing what he knew and keeping a confidence. Professional integrity—or maybe simple habit—won. "From what I've learned, Robert's stuck to the same story no matter who he talks to."

The sheriff nodded. "Figured as much. Did he say

anything about them fellas he's been runnin' with lately?''

"Not much," Nathan told him truthfully.

"Uh-huh." The sheriff rubbed his chin and contemplated his next words. "Well, let me tell you what I know. A few of 'em are from around here. Go to school with Robert. Good kids, basically."

"That's what I understand."

"It's the others I'm concerned about."

"Others?"

"Imports from around Atlanta." His eyebrows drew together in a concerned frown. "Bad news. Particularly the leader. Believe his name's Gus Anderson."

The knot in Nathan's gut tightened. Rawlins was confirming his own suspicions that there might be gang activity in the area. This added a whole new dimension to the potential danger to Robert. And to Rachel. Not to mention the whole town.

Nathan knew how gangs worked. He'd seen enough of them in inner cities, seen the misery they could cause. They zeroed in on the weaknesses in local authority figures, then set out to bring them down. After that, they went after the innocents.

"What do you think their interest is up here?" Nathan wanted to see if Rawlins was still as shrewd as he remembered.

"I've asked myself the same question. We're relatively close to Atlanta, just shy a hundred miles north. There're a couple of small colleges down the road, lots of good-looking girls. Local boys they can recruit. I'd say they wanna be big fishes in a little pond." He scratched his chin again and eyed Nathan. "That about how you'd size it up?"

"What makes you think I'm qualified to give an

opinion about gangs?'' Nathan asked, still hoping not to be pulled into the town's troubles. But he knew it was too late. Rawlins might be as sharp as ever, but he was past his prime, physically out of shape, ready for retirement. He wouldn't stand a chance against this new threat.

And Rawlins had his number. Nathan had always felt an unreasonable responsibility toward Rachel. It had begun one hot Georgia summer afternoon when he'd walked into his parents' living room to find a solemn, defiant young Rachel sitting on the sofa. It had become stronger as their friendship grew and deepened. He was learning that the years away from her hadn't shaken it.

''Now, son,'' the sheriff chided, ''I kept in touch with your mama, rest her soul, before she passed on. She told me all 'bout the work you been doing the last few years up there in Washington, D.C. I figure you know a whole lot more'n I do.''

''I appreciate your vote of confidence.'' Nathan exhaled deeply. ''But why are you telling me this?''

''Robert's right at that age when he could go either way. Thought you might be interested, seeing as how you and his sister go back a long way.''

Nathan knew when he'd been bested by an expert. The only thing left was to accept defeat gracefully. ''Thanks for the information.''

Sheriff Rawlins patted him on the shoulder. ''I know you'll do the right thing.'' He gave Nathan a farewell salute. ''Good seeing you again, son. Hope you'll stick around for a while.''

Nathan watched the sheriff saunter through the hospital doors. It looked as though he wasn't going to have much choice.

* * *

Several days later, Nathan pulled the Harley to a stop in front of Rachel's house. It was a perfect April morning—cloudless sky, gentle breeze, the fulfillment of the promise for a new beginning. He took a moment to appreciate the beauty of nature's renewal, wondering why things couldn't be as simple for man.

Providence seemed hell-bent on thrusting him into Rachel's life. The last thing he wanted was to assume responsibility for another soul. His track record was lousy. He hadn't been able to keep his own brother safe. Why would anyone think he could do a better job with Robert?

And what, Nathan wondered, would it do to Rachel if he failed?

But he knew Rachel, knew what Robert meant to her. He'd already seen a sample of how far she was willing to go to help him. If he walked away from this, he wouldn't put it past her to try something even more dangerous than what she'd done his first night back in town.

Rachel Holcomb had always had a little too much guts and not enough common sense. She'd walk into a hornets' nest in the belief that she could reason with them. But he'd never seen her commit a violent act in all the time he'd known her. Having spent her younger years in a home where violence could be a daily occurrence, he knew how much she abhorred it.

The knot of uneasiness in his gut wouldn't go away. No matter how he'd rationalized over the past several days, he couldn't escape the inescapable: He had no choice, but to get involved. At least for as long as he was in town.

He consoled himself with the promise that it wouldn't be that much longer. His business in Thunder Ridge was almost finished. The house would be ready to go on the market within a few weeks. How complicated could things get in that length of time? It was a weak attempt at reassurance, but it was the best he could do.

He got off the bike and slowly climbed the steps to Rachel's front porch.

Rachel opened the door on the second knock. It took her a moment to register that it was Nathan Garner standing on the other side. Dressed in leather, his hair mussed from the motorcycle helmet, he looked absurdly attractive.

"What are you doing here?"

"You're going to have to work on your greetings," he said, his blue eyes teasing. "Or I might get the impression you're not glad to see me."

She recalled their last meeting and how it ended. "I think you have that backward." Folding her arms, she leaned against the doorjamb, blocking his path into the house. "This is Monday. How'd you know I'd be home?"

"I called your clinic," he said. "They told me you'd taken the day off." His gaze skimmed the length of her.

Since the day promised to be unseasonably warm even for late April in Georgia, she'd slipped on a bright red knit top and short shorts. Now she felt a ridiculous urge to tug them down an inch or three.

"How resourceful. So I'll ask again, what are you doing here?"

"It's a nice day. Thought you might like to take a ride."

Her gaze drifted to the motorcycle parked in the drive, and she blinked twice. "On *that?*"

"The other night at the hospital you told me you

didn't understand Robert.'' He gestured to the bike. ''The best way to start is by understanding what he loves.''

She wondered if this meant Nathan had changed his mind about getting involved in Robert's problems. She welcomed the possibility at the same time she found it unsettling. As she eyed the bike, gratitude warred with apprehension. Motorcycles had never been among her favorite forms of transportation.

''Right now?''

''Robert's in school today, isn't he?''

''Yes.''

He cocked his head. ''Is there a better time?''

''My vote would be in another life,'' she said dryly. ''But I guess you wouldn't come all the way over here if you didn't think it was important.''

A grin spread across his face, and her stomach did a little flip-flop. ''Good guess.''

''That's what I figured.'' She sighed in resignation. ''Okay, let's get it over with.''

''Such enthusiasm.'' His grin widened. ''Much as I hate to mention it,'' he said regretfully, again scanning her attire, ''you need to change clothes.'' His gaze moved to her mouth and lingered a moment.

''Oh.'' She glanced down at herself, then her gaze swung up to meet his. ''What should I wear?''

''Something in leather—'' he wiggled his eyebrows suggestively ''—if you have it.''

Sensual awareness fluttered through her, and to compensate she sent him a chiding look. ''Why leather?''

''It gives the best protection…in case we take a fall.''

She shivered. ''That doesn't sound very reassuring.''

''Just taking precautions,'' he told her. ''If you don't have leather, denim is a passable second choice.''

"I'll see what I can find."

A short while later she returned, wearing an old pair of leather pants she'd forgotten she still had and one of Robert's jackets.

"I just don't get it," she grumbled, eyeing the motorcycle as she approached it uneasily. "What's to love about riding this thing at breakneck speed and getting bugs stuck in your teeth?"

Chuckling, he handed her a helmet. "Here, put this on. Your teeth are safe."

Her teeth might be safe, she thought ruefully, but what about the rest of her? "Where are we going?"

"You'll see." He helped her with the helmet, then showed her how to mount and where to sit. "Watch the tail pipes," he cautioned, pointing them out. "They can burn you."

She wondered if that was the only thing here today that had the power to burn her.

Once she was settled and he'd given her some basic instructions on what was expected of a passenger, he started the engine. Surprisingly, from this position his bike had a rich deep purr to it—loud, but somehow pleasant. It vibrated through her, filling her with an almost erotic sensation.

He twisted his head to look back at her. "Ready?" he shouted through the visor of his dark helmet.

She nodded her reluctant agreement, wishing she could see his face, read his expression.

Pulling her arms snugly around him, he anchored her hands at his waist. "Hold on tight."

Within minutes they were roaring down the highway at what seemed like the speed of light. The wind whipped past them, yanking at her clothing as if trying to tear each piece from her body. Reflexively, her fingers clutched two handfuls of leather at Nathan's waist, and she pressed herself more snugly against his back.

His solid form helped shield her from the worst of the wind, and she began to draw courage from him. She became aware of his confidence in handling the powerful machine and experienced the first tingle of exhilaration as he leaned into the turns, taking her with him. It was, she decided, almost like an exotic dance.

Traffic was light, but whenever they passed another motorcycle, Nathan signaled a greeting. It added a pleasant note of camaraderie with other bikers. Slowly she began to notice the landscape racing past them, the profusion of colors, the smell of wildflowers. The heat of the sun on her back seeped through her jacket, enticing her to relax and savor the experience. By the time they reached their destination, her senses were humming.

Nathan shut off the engine, and the roar of the bike was replaced by the loud rush of water cascading down steep mountain rocks. She took in her surroundings, startled to discover that he'd brought her to Thunder Falls. He'd first brought her here shortly after she'd moved into the Garner household and explained that it was from these falls that the town got its name.

During her teenage years, whenever he was home from college on breaks, they'd come up here often to gaze at the falls and talk. This was where she'd learned so much about Nathan's hopes and dreams. Where she'd revealed many of her own. Where they'd fallen in love.

Where he'd asked her to marry him.

A sharp ache darted through her as she recalled the last time she'd been here—and what had transpired. She wondered if he'd forgotten.

Nathan kicked the bike stand into position and, without disturbing her, swung his leg over the front of the Harley and stood. Once he'd removed his helmet, he offered her a hand. ''Need some help?''

''Please,'' she said, deciding she and her wobbly legs could use all the assistance they could get. He gently pulled her helmet off, then led her over to a large rock that offered a breathtaking view of the falls. With a sigh she removed her jacket, settled herself on the warm surface and encircled her updrawn knees with her arms.

He stretched out beside her, not touching her, but close enough that her overstimulated senses were acutely attuned to him. He reminded her of some mythic pagan god, rather than a minister. She mentally shook her head at the whimsical notion.

''So. What do you think of your first bike ride?'' he asked after several minutes of silence.

''You mean once I got over the initial terror?''

For the first time since he'd been back, genuine humor warmed his eyes. ''Something like that.''

His smile was infectious. ''Not as bad as I expected. A little exciting,'' she said grudgingly. ''A lot scary.''

''But did you enjoy it?''

She wasn't sure *enjoy* was the right word, although her apprehension had vanished once she'd gotten the hang of it. ''I will admit I have a better idea why Robert finds it so appealing.''

He chuckled. ''That sounds promising.''

She glanced over at him, taking pleasure in the fact that he seemed more relaxed. With a pang of longing she acknowledged how much she'd missed him, missed their easy companionship, his quiet understanding. Careful, a corner of her heart cautioned.

''Tell me, what is it that you love about it?''

Rachel's question caught him unprepared, and Nathan considered his answer before speaking. "There's an aspect of danger in bike riding that makes you more aware of things around you."

She turned so that she faced him. "In what way?"

Propping himself on one elbow, he stared out at the water's relentless rush to its destination at the bottom of the falls. It helped dilute some of the effect Rachel's closeness was having on him.

"It clears my head. There's something almost spiritual about it—as if for that span of time, I'm in tune with nature." He paused. "I think what I love most is the sense of freedom, the feeling that I can go wherever the wind takes me."

"In other words," she said, "it represents a means of escape."

He thought about that. "Yes, I suppose it does." As she'd done so many times in the past, she'd found the heart of it.

She squinted against the sun's glare. "Do you think that's how Robert looks at it?"

"It's hard to say," he told her. "Riding a bike affects different people in different ways. But I'd say he feels some of the same things."

She nodded. "And his…friends, they probably feel the same?"

"Probably." He picked up a new leaf that had somehow been torn from a tree before having a chance to fully develop. "There's nothing inherently bad about motorcycles," he told her. "There're a lot of good people who love them. From professionals to lay people—doctors, lawyers, teachers…"

"Even ministers," she finished for him, and smiled. "The rational side of me realizes that. It's the other side that keeps reminding me of the dangers. The bad apples.''

"Robert's trying to discover who he is." He wondered just how candid she wanted him to be. "At the moment the idea of getting involved with this group seems exciting," he said, deliberately not using the word *gang*.

"So, what do I do? Ordering him to stay away from them doesn't seem to work."

He nodded in sympathy, understanding her frustration. "He needs to be weaned away from their influence. Find a substitute to keep him busy. Something that he'll enjoy and get interested in. Robert's a good kid. He'll come around."

"I pray you're right." She sent him a considering look. "How do you know so much about teenagers?"

"It's called survival. You either learn what makes them tick and how to stay ahead of them, or they'll trample you on their way out the door."

Amusement softened her features. "Tell me about your work."

He should have been prepared for that. Rachel had always been good at catching him off guard, digging beneath the surface. He didn't want to open this discussion because he knew it could open up painful areas. But he doubted she'd let it drop.

"That's a pretty broad subject."

"I'm certain," she said, watching him steadily, "that you can find a way to summarize."

How did he go about summarizing something so complicated? He leaned back and closed his eyes. "Most recently I've been working with inner-city kids. Trying to help them find an alternative to life on the streets."

"In Washington?"

"Yes."

"As a minister?"

"A rather unconventional one, but yes," he said with a self-deprecating laugh. "It's a nondenominational ministry, so we make up the rules as we go along."

She chuckled, and he thought again how much he'd missed the sound of it.

"Haven't you always? If you're not part of an established denomination, where do you get the money to run it?"

"The goodwill of various religious organizations and private donors who support our cause."

"What about government agencies?"

"We try to stay away from those. Too many strings, too much red tape. Besides, if these kids get wind of any kind of bureaucratic authority, they run like hell."

"Why?"

"Living on the streets has taught them that it's not wise to trust anyone."

"But they trust you," she said quietly.

"Some do. Most don't." He shifted restlessly, thinking of the endless list of needs that could never be met, the problems begging for impossible solutions. And the kids, jaded beyond their years, too aware of those facts.

"You must have had some victories."

"A few," he said. "But never enough. There's so much to do. And no one can do it all."

"And is it dangerous?" she asked, a slight frown furrowing her brow.

He thought of the kids who'd been wounded or killed, the ones who flirted with death by using drugs. He thought of the kid he'd just lost.

"Sometimes," he prevaricated, not wanting to discuss any of this with Rachel.

Concern darkened her eyes. "Is there nothing that can be done?"

"Lots of things are being tried." He grimaced. "But there's no easy solution. So many of these kids don't appreciate the sanctity of human life. And if they don't value life to begin with, it becomes too easy to destroy it."

"I guess that would be enough to cause someone to leave...even the ministry." Her words were spoken softly, as if directed to herself rather than him. But he heard the unspoken questions.

How did he explain to her that he was burned out, emotionally drained? First he'd failed his own brother. Then he'd failed someone else, a younger man, one who many people had said wasn't worth his effort. But Nathan had seen something good in him, had tried to nurture it. He'd succeeded to a degree, until the kid had succumbed to the seductive lure of drugs and street life.

"Thanks for telling me," Rachel said when he remained silent for several minutes. "And thanks for the crash course in motorcycles," she added, changing the subject. She grinned. "No pun intended. I think I understand Robert a little better now."

"You're welcome," he said, grateful that she'd decided to back off the subject. "Glad it helped."

"I realize you'd rather not get involved in Robert's problems. I don't know what changed your mind, but I appreciate anything you're willing to do. Including anything that sheds light on the inner workings of the teenage male."

He wanted to tell her not to pin her hopes on him. She might end up being disappointed. "Don't expect too much,'' he said instead. ''I'm only here for a few more weeks. I won't promise anything, but I'll do what I can.''

''Thank you for that.'' She studied him. ''You've changed, you know. You're nothing like I remember.''

He thought he caught a trace of sadness in her eyes. ''Most people change,'' he told her guardedly. ''It comes with living.''

''That's one explanation.''

Her continued scrutiny unsettled him, and he sat up. ''Maybe your memories aren't accurate.''

''Maybe they're not.'' She sighed. ''Perhaps I created my own fantasy.''

That was what worried him. He'd had only a year with Rachel before he'd left for college, then divinity school. But during that year they'd shared the same house; he'd learned more about her dreams than most men could in a lifetime. He also knew her fantasies.

''I'm not who you think I am, Rachel,'' he told her gently. ''I never have been.''

''So you've said before.''

She still insisted on seeing things in him that he knew weren't there. From the beginning he'd struggled with a deep dread that once she discovered the *real* Nathan Garner, she couldn't possibly love him. He wasn't the gentle, patient man she seemed to think he was. If he saw something that needed doing, he did it—and worried about the consequences later. His own father and brother had had trouble understanding him. How could Rachel be any different?

She looked delicious sitting there, so serious, with the wind ruffling strands of her hair that had escaped the heavy braid. He wondered if she still tasted as sweet as he remembered. With effort, he dragged his thoughts away from those memories and searched for another topic.

"I'm surprised you're not married."

She looked as stunned as he felt by the comment, but she recovered quickly. "Why? Is my time running out?"

He should have known better than to open that discussion. He wasn't ready for where it might lead. He shrugged, pretending nothing more than friendly interest. "I figured by now you'd have a houseful of kids."

"Well, the thing is, that requires a man to be their father." She looked at him, her gaze steady. "And I never found another candidate as good as you."

He struggled to catch his breath and hang on to his composure. Her straightforward honesty had, on more than one occasion, affected him like a boxer's punch to the solar plexus. That hadn't changed. Except this time it held a sensual impact as well.

He'd been aching to kiss her ever since she'd opened the door this morning, looking as fresh and promising as spring. And wearing shorts that defined the term, making him painfully aware of her long, long legs.

"Oh, Rachel. It's a mistake to tempt me," he said gruffly. "I might be a minister, but I'm still a flesh-and-blood man."

As if to prove the point, he caught hold of her hand and tugged her to him. He managed to temper the fire raging through him a split second before his mouth settled over hers.

Chapter Eight

Nathan's kiss was as intense as Rachel remembered, though tinged with a dark eroticism not present six years ago. It was as if his emotions had been held in check all this time, waiting for this moment to be released. She welcomed the taste and feel of him, unable to get enough. It had been so long! But she sensed his ever-present self-control, though barely held in check. She'd always resented that tight control. Feeling reckless, she deepened the kiss, challenging it—challenging him.

With a guttural groan, he fell back, pulling her down on top of him. She was instantly aware of the heat of his arousal pressed intimately against her. He crushed her against him, making certain she felt its full extent. There was a raw hunger in him that she instinctively knew couldn't be satisfied with mere kisses—even ones as potent as these.

A trickle of anxiety raced through her, along with mounting sexual excitement. What had possessed her, she wondered, to tease a tiger in its cage?

It was the cry of a hawk circling overhead that finally penetrated Nathan's sensual fog. He jerked upright, pulling Rachel with him. What in heaven's name was the matter with him? He had no right to kiss her—and certainly not here. This spot might be relatively secluded, but it was still a public place, unprotected, where anyone could wander up. Rachel deserved better. She deserved tenderness and respect.

She deserved better than him.

"I'm…sorry." He shoved both hands through his hair, noting the tremor in them. He should have realized that coming to the falls was a mistake. There were too many memories here. "I shouldn't have done that."

Beside him Rachel took a deep, shuddering breath. He was doing it to her again. "What?" she said, trying to make her voice light. "Kiss me, or stop kissing me?"

He stared at her for the space of a heartbeat. "Both," he said succinctly, then got to his feet and walked over to the bike.

Rachel wondered whether an old-fashioned temper tantrum would make her feel any better. Before Nathan had left for the far-off country that had seemed like the ends of the earth to her romantic nineteen-year-old mind, she'd begged him to make love to her only a short distance from here. But he'd gently refused, his perfect control keeping them in check. She'd yearned for that one memory to hold close all the lonely days and nights while he was gone. But he'd held her off while chaining her to him, body and soul.

Now she was allowing him to do it to her all over again.

"We need to get back," he called to her after a bit.

She agreed. She needed to get away from him before she said or did something she might regret. She grabbed her jacket and pulled it on, before joining him beside the bike.

He handed her the helmet and nodded toward the bike. "You want to take her for a spin?" he said, as if nothing out of the ordinary had just transpired between them.

Fine. If he wanted to act as if nothing happened, she could oblige. "Me?" she asked dubiously. "By myself?"

He chuckled, but without the earlier humor. "I promise I'll be right behind you."

"What would be the point?"

Nathan wanted to tell Rachel it would give him an excuse to hold her when he couldn't come up with another rational one. "Because riding is only half the thrill," he told her instead. "And I want you to experience what it's like to be in control."

"Why not?" She took the helmet from him and put it on. "I might as well get the full treatment. Maybe it will clear my head. It certainly needs it."

She had trouble jump-starting the bike, so eventually Nathan had to start it for her. Once the powerful machine was rumbling contentedly, he helped her on and guided her hands to the handlebars. Without words, he showed her how to steer and work the throttle. Then he settled himself on the seat behind her.

Being cradled between Nathan's strong thighs was both distracting and arousing. It opened up a whole new realm of sensations not unlike those she'd experienced on their ride up to the falls. But this was far more erotic.

As they pulled away, she was all too aware of him

pressed against her back, a comforting presence should she need his aid. She had to force herself to concentrate on the road.

Getting involved with Nathan Garner again, she silently warned herself, was out of the question.

She couldn't afford to open up old wounds. That held too much pain.

She had to think of her brother. Robert needed Nathan's help. Her *brother* was the most important person in her life now.

But something told her she could only fool herself for so long.

I'll be around. Those had been Nathan's last words to Rachel when he'd dropped her off at her house Monday afternoon. Today was Friday and she hadn't seen him since. But he'd been as good as his word. Every afternoon while she was still at work, he'd picked up Robert and taken him over to the Garner place to help with odd jobs. And, she was sure, to work on the motorcycle. Each evening about suppertime he dropped Robert off at the door.

The sound of a car motor interrupted her thoughts. She placed the box of picnic supplies she'd been collecting on the hall table. Glancing out the front window, she saw Robert climb out of Nathan's van, give a wave and slam the door. The van backed out of the drive, the setting sun reflecting off its windshield. She caught only the briefest glimpse of Nathan as he drove away.

Her heart squeezed in disappointment, and she silently chastised herself for noticing that for the fourth night in a row he hadn't come in. He was doing what he said he'd do—help Robert. The fact that she and

Nathan had shared a soul-shattering kiss didn't obligate him to do anything more.

Robert bounded up the steps and through the front door.

"Hey, Rach, what's happening?" He snagged an apple from the box she'd just set down.

"Ah, good," she said, striving to sound upbeat. "You're just in time." Thankfully his bruises had all faded, and the cut on his jaw would leave only a slight scar.

"Just in time for what?" He surveyed the boxes stacked neatly on the floor near the front door.

"To help me load these in the car."

"What's all this stuff for?"

Robert munched happily, while Rachel lifted her eyes heavenward and prayed for patience. "For the church outing tomorrow. Remember? White-water rafting. Kids. Food. Fun."

Her brother's munching slowed. "Oh, that," he said. "I forgot."

Rachel turned to look at him and frowned. He was shuffling his feet, which wasn't promising. Nathan's advice had been to wean Robert away from his current group of friends by getting him involved in another activity. She'd figured rafting would be a good start. It was beginning to appear that she might have figured wrong.

"Well, consider yourself reminded. Grab a box. I have to get this over to the church tonight."

He made no move to comply. "Nathan didn't say anything about going rafting."

She opened the door and picked up a box. "Why would he?"

Robert shrugged. "I dunno. If it's so great, why wouldn't he be going?"

"Maybe he has something else to do." Exasperation was beginning to get the better of her. "It'll be fun, you'll see."

He set his chin stubbornly. "Nah, I'm not interested."

"Why not?"

"Because only wimps are interested in something that dorky."

"How would you know? You've never been rafting." She sighed, conceding that she'd lost this battle. She'd have to devise another plan of attack. "Grab a box," she told him again. "Whether you go or not, these things need to get over to the church. And they won't get there by themselves."

Robert laid his half-eaten apple on the table, half-heartedly picked up a box and followed her out to the car.

Nathan parked his van at the curb of the main street running through Thunder Ridge's bustling business district. As he stepped down from the vehicle, he paused to look around the familiar area. Not much had changed over the years. Like most small municipalities in this part of the country, this one had its requisite town square with a courthouse, sheriff's office, post office, bank, a few struggling stores and, in one corner, a church.

He looked up at the old wooden church building. It had been his father's until his death. While growing up, Nathan, his brother and any foster children staying with the family had spent a good share of their time there.

Long before he'd ever made the difficult decision to

enter the ministry, Nathan had secretly longed to be good enough to head a church like this. But he'd known it could never be this particular one. This one required someone with his father's gentle authority or his brother Matthew's naive belief in the inherent goodness of mankind.

That belief had been the cause of Matthew's death. But Nathan was ultimately to blame. He should have protected his brother. Nathan, always the pragmatic one, knew that sometimes mankind needed a kick in the butt to point it in the right direction.

His gaze followed the church spire that reached toward a startlingly blue sky. Matthew's death had badly shaken his faith. After that failure, he'd managed to find some solace in trying to salvage inner-city street kids. He'd chosen that ministry because it suited his personality.

He knew how to deal with kids on the streets. Hell, at times while he was growing up, Sheriff Rawlins had been convinced Nathan was one step away from becoming a juvenile deliquent. The unconventional ministry had seemed the logical choice after his brother's death. He'd wanted to make a difference, wanted to help. But he'd failed again. Not only had he lost his brother, he'd been unable to save a kid who'd never had a chance at a decent life. A kid he'd thought he'd managed to rescue.

Now he'd come home, doubting that he was equipped to serve any ministry. With effort he shook off the heavy thoughts. He jogged up the granite steps and around the side of the building to the door that led to the minister's study. A sign on the door read Come In.

Before entering, he tugged at the tie he wasn't accustomed to wearing. He'd put it on, along with the dress shirt, in deference to the memory of his mother and the hours she'd spent drilling her sons on proper church attire. His one concession to comfort was his casual trousers. He rapped once and opened the door.

Paul McDaniel looked up from behind the large desk that had once belonged to Nathan's father and smiled. "Nathan," he said, getting to his feet and coming around the desk to welcome him. "Thank you for stopping by on such short notice." He gestured to a chair.

"No problem." Nathan took the proffered seat. "I was planning to be in town today anyway." During Paul's call to him late last night, he had mentioned something about Nathan picking up a few of his father's things that had been overlooked since his death.

Paul nodded at the medium-size cardboard box sitting on one corner of the desk. "This is it. Not much to speak of. A few books, some files, a couple of knick-knacks. Since you appear to be closing out your life here," he said, returning to his seat and folding his hands in front of him on the desk, "I thought you might want to take these with you."

Nathan looked at the other man sharply, uncertain whether he'd detected a note of censure hidden in the minister's otherwise friendly words. But his expression remained benign.

"This is the most interesting item," he continued, picking up a small metal box and pushing it across the desk toward Nathan.

Nathan picked it up, one side of his mouth lifting in a smile. "I haven't seen this in years." As far back as he could remember, the box had been among his father's possessions. The size of a cigar box, it had long ago lost most of its black enamel paint. As a kid, he'd tried to imagine what wonderful secrets it might hold. He tested the lock, but it held fast. "Is there a key?"

"I didn't run across one. But it shouldn't be difficult to find a substitute that will work."

Frowning slightly, Nathan set the box aside, surprised at the disappointment he experienced. "Thanks for saving this for me," he said quietly.

"You're welcome," Paul replied, eyes suddenly twinkling. "I hope this means you won't mind if I ask a favor in return."

"What kind of favor?"

He glanced at his watch and grimaced. "In about an hour, I'm supposed to help chaperon a bunch of hellions on our annual spring rafting excursion."

Nathan grinned at the older man's colorful language and comical expression. "And how does a favor figure in?"

"I'm getting too old for that kind of…fun." He looked pleadingly at Nathan. "Could I persuade you to go in my place?"

Nathan's grin turned wry. He didn't intend to become caught up in the local church again. It stirred too many mixed emotions. A part of him felt at home here, as if this was where he belonged. But he knew that couldn't be. He'd never truly belonged here. Or anywhere.

"The day you're too old to work with kids, we'll all be in trouble." Nathan got to his feet, recognizing that he was being manipulated. "I wish I could help you out, but I have several errands to run." He wondered if he'd be struck by lightning for fibbing to a minister in his church study.

Paul looked momentarily crestfallen, but he rallied quickly. "Ah, well," he said philosophically, then came around the desk. "You can't blame me for trying. Come on. I'll walk you out."

Instead of using the side door, Paul ushered Nathan through the one that led to the interior of the church. As they stepped out of the office, an outside door burst open to admit several young people dressed for rafting. They called greetings to Paul, then clattered downstairs to the activity room below the main sanctuary. When the door opened again, Rachel walked through, carrying a duffel bag.

The sudden jolt to his heart startled him. He'd thought he was long past that kind of reaction to a beautiful woman. But, a tiny corner of his heart whispered, this wasn't just *any* beautiful woman. This was Rachel.

He tried to suppress the memory of the last time he'd seen her. And the kiss they'd shared. She'd been so responsive—giving, sweet, warm. Loving. All the things missing in his life for so long.

Feeling his body's response, he realized he was in serious trouble if he didn't find something else to focus on. The fact that Rachel was wearing shorts and a T-shirt didn't help any—even if they would be considered modest by the most conservative standards. He scowled, wondering how many other males would have the same reaction.

For once, fate seemed to be on his side. Robert came through the door seconds behind Rachel, giving Nathan something else to concentrate on.

"Oh, good," Paul said to Nathan, "Robert did come, after all."

He might be here, Nathan thought, but the boy looked less than enthusiastic at the prospect.

"He appears to be doing better," Paul continued. "I

think working with you is helping. I know Rachel is pleased.''

Nathan shifted uneasily. ''Her optimism may be premature. We'll see what happens down the road.'' That was what had concerned him—Rachel expecting too much, setting herself up for disappointment. ''Robert's a good kid, but there's no way to predict what's going on in his head.''

''Have a little faith, son,'' Paul admonished kindly. ''You're doing the right thing.''

Nathan shook his head and smiled wryly. Someone had been expecting him to do the right thing his entire life. And it was still as complicated as it was difficult. It never came with easy solutions—or simple choices.

And he knew from painful experience that success was never guaranteed.

Rachel looked over her shoulder to see if Robert had followed her. She was relieved to see him come through the door. Their heated debate in the car on the way to the church had left little doubt where her brother stood on the subject of rafting.

As she turned to start down the stairs to the activity room, her gaze connected with Nathan's. Even across the width of the room, he held her frozen. The shock of seeing him startled her so much that she almost missed the first step. Dressed in a crisp white shirt and conservative tie, he looked ready to step up to the pulpit and deliver a sermon.

A vast difference from the last time she'd seen him.

That memory heated her face with embarrassment, followed closely by irritation that he could make her feel like an awkward schoolgirl encountering her lover after an illicit rendezvous. For some reason, it seemed vital that she not allow Nathan to guess her reaction.

"Here," she said to Robert, handing him the duffel bag she'd been carrying. "Please take these supplies downstairs. I'll be down in a few minutes."

Robert grumbled, but thankfully didn't argue. Squaring her shoulders, she walked over to where Nathan stood next to Paul McDaniel.

"Hi," she said, her greeting including both men.

Paul responded first. "Good morning, Rachel." He rubbed his hands together. "Ah, well," he continued, when no one else spoke, "I have things to do. I'll leave you two alone." He gave an abbreviated wave and ducked back inside his office.

Nathan didn't speak until the door closed. "How are you?"

Why did his voice have to sound so deep...so seductive? "Fine," she said a bit too brightly.

"What are you doing at church on a Saturday morning?"

"I'm helping with last-minute preparations for the outing." She wondered if she sounded breathless to him.

He studied her a moment. "How's Robert?"

Glancing around, she realized her brother had apparently followed her instructions and headed downstairs. "Not particularly interested in being here," she said, frustration creasing her forehead.

"Why's that?"

"I think it has something to do with his opinion that rafting is dorky."

Nathan chuckled. "Where'd he get that idea?"

"He wasn't very specific, but I think his reasoning

runs along the lines that if *you're* not going, then it can't be that much fun.''

That seemed to surprise him. ''Me? What do I have to do with it?''

''You understand the workings of a teenager's mind better than I do.''

His gaze shifted to the stairway down which Robert had disappeared, then back to her. Shaking his head, he smiled crookedly. ''That's one mystery no one will ever understand. Do you want me to talk to him?''

Something told her that he was hoping she'd say no. But no matter how much she might want to, she couldn't let him off the hook. If anyone could talk sense to her brother, it was Nathan. She smiled almost apologetically. ''I really would appreciate it.''

She thought she caught a look of momentary panic darken his eyes before he said, ''I'll go find him and see what I can do.''

Nathan found Robert downstairs near the staging area for the outing. Several kids, supervised by a handful of adults, were helping to load supplies into vans parked just outside the wide doors. Arms folded across his chest, Robert stood alone, leaning against a wall out of the hustle and bustle. Wearing grungy jeans, an oversize shirt and sneakers, he definitely wasn't dressed for rafting. When he spotted Nathan, his expression lost some of its sulkiness.

''Rachel tells me you're not interested in going rafting,'' Nathan said conversationally, propping himself against the same wall.

''Nah, not much.''

Nathan noticed that Robert was watching the preparations intently. ''Why is that?''

One of Robert's shoulders lifted and fell in a careless shrug. "It's for sissies."

"You think so?"

"Yeah." Robert looked at him. "Don't you?"

"Have you ever been down the river?"

The teenager shook his head.

"Too bad. It's almost as exciting as riding a motorcycle. Maybe even more."

Robert looked surprised but doubtful. "Yeah? So you've done it?"

"Hundreds of times, while I was growing up."

For several moments Robert digested that bit of information. Finally he said, "I still don't want to."

"Well, I think you're safe. Doesn't look like anyone's trying to force you."

"Except for Rachel," he muttered. "Do many bikers go rafting?"

"What has that got to do with it?"

"Well...I don't want the guys to get any stupid ideas about me."

"What kind of ideas?"

Robert looked uncomfortable. "That I'm a wimp...or a sissy—" he shrugged "—y'know..."

Nathan was beginning to get the picture. Robert wanted to be considered tough, which meant that he didn't want any of his friends getting wind of him doing something that wasn't considered cool. But to be weaned away from that particular group, Robert needed to discover something else that interested him. And that wasn't going to happen if he was allowed to shy away from anything he feared might be less than cool.

"Yeah, well," Nathan said, realizing he was speaking to himself as much as Robert, "sometimes we all have to take chances."

"Huh?"

"Rachel seems to have her heart set on you giving this rafting thing a shot. And since you owe her—and me…" He let the thought trail off, subtly reminding Robert of his broken promise not to cause his sister any more grief.

"Aw, man!" Robert sent Nathan a disgusted look. "I shoulda figured. You're going to blackmail me again."

"Hey." Nathan held up his hands unapologetically. "It's your call."

"Yeah, right," he grumbled. "Oh, okay, I'll go."

"Smart decision."

"You think so because you don't have to live with it."

"Sometimes taking a chance is worth the risk." Nathan gave him a comforting pat on the back. "You do know how to swim, don't you?" Being a certified swimmer was a basic requirement to participate.

Robert looked slightly insulted. "Of course," he said, leaving the words *doesn't everyone?* unspoken. He took a closer look at Nathan. "Are you gonna wear *those* clothes?"

"Oh, I'm not going," Nathan said. "I've got things to do in town."

"No way, man." A wicked grin spread across Robert's face. "If *I* gotta go, *you* gotta go."

It was difficult, but Nathan managed to hide his smile. The kid was clever. "Deal," he said, conceding without a fight. What choice did he have? He was already committed to helping Robert. "Let's go find Rachel, then see what we can dig up to wear."

But Rachel found them first, spotting them as she came down the stairs. "Hi," she said, coming to a stop in front of them, looking from one to the other. "Everything okay?"

"Just peachy," Robert said with just a touch of sarcasm.

"*We*'re on our way to change clothes," Nathan explained pointedly.

He noticed that Rachel did a valiant job of not jumping up and down and clapping her hands. "Oh. Well. That's wonderful," she said, smiling broadly. "I guess I'll see you guys at the pickup point when you're finished."

"What do you mean, pickup point?" Nathan asked. "Aren't you planning to go?"

She smiled sweetly and shook her head.

Nathan looked at her with a gleam of retribution in his eyes. "Oh, yes, you are. You got me into this, lady. If *we* go," he said, paraphrasing Robert's earlier challenge, "*you* go."

Chapter Nine

The old Myers bridge was just as Rachel remembered. How many times had she and Nathan launched a raft from the sandy beach beside this very bridge and floated the couple of miles to the pickup point downstream? She wondered if he ever thought of those times.

She inhaled the fresh spring air. It was a perfect day. The sky was a bottomless blue, and though only early May, the weather was as hot as July but without the mugginess.

An assortment of adults and kids piled out of the vans, noisily pitching in to get the rafts unloaded and down to the river's edge. Required dress for these outings was either some sort of modified wetsuit or other protective clothing to guard against the dazzling sun, chilly water and abrasive rocks.

Luckily Nathan had been able to borrow appropriate clothing for Robert and himself. And despite herself,

Rachel couldn't keep from noticing the way Nathan's abbreviated wet suit hugged his broad back and slim hips. Or her reaction to it. She couldn't seem to stop herself from envisioning him without that suit. Mentally she shook herself. What in the world had triggered these X-rated thoughts?

"Okay, listen up!" Nathan yelled above the rush of the river and the clamor of voices.

Everyone quieted and looked at him expectantly.

"For those of you who don't know me, my name's Nathan. Reverend McDaniel asked me to fill in for him this morning."

The group mumbled their acceptance of the change in plans.

"Most of you know the drill. Everyone who's been rafting before, go stand over there." He indicated the sandy area near the rafts. "Everyone else come over here beside me."

Standing a couple of feet behind him, Rachel smiled inwardly, knowing Nathan was still trying to figure out how he'd come to be in charge. He couldn't seem to accept the fact that he was the obvious choice.

Only Robert sauntered over to stand next to him. "Geez, take out an ad, why doncha," she heard him mutter to Nathan.

"Didn't mean to embarrass you," Nathan said, keeping his voice equally low. "I figured there'd be a few others."

The youngest member of the group, a little girl around six years old with golden hair and dark brown eyes, came over to Robert and tugged on his sleeve. "Hi," she said brightly. "My name is Becky Lynn Adams. What's yours?"

"Robert," he answered. Grudgingly.

''The rule says if you haven't been rafting before, you have to go with someone who has,'' she explained.

Robert folded his arms. ''Is that so.''

She nodded, her expression earnest. ''I've been lots of times, so I can be your buddy,'' she said, beaming up at him. ''That way, you won't have to worry. *I'll* take care of you.''

Robert's ears turned a dull red, and he looked as if he wished he were anywhere but here. Rachel held her breath, waiting for his reaction.

''Thanks,'' he mumbled to Becky Lynn and shot Nathan a look that promised a reckoning. Soon.

''Good job,'' Nathan told Robert quietly, then in a louder voice he said, ''Okay, folks, let's get these rafts in the water.''

Amid squeals and shouts, everyone hustled to comply. Nathan issued last-minute safety instructions, while Rachel and the other adults checked helmets and life jackets. In the resulting flurry of activity, no one had time to pay attention to her brother. Nathan had managed to resolve the situation without further embarrassment.

Nathan obviously enjoyed the kids almost as much as she knew he enjoyed the sport. Even Becky Lynn, who seemed capable of talking nonstop, didn't bother him. Rachel watched him patiently answer what had to be the child's hundredth question of the day. And everyone present appeared to enjoy him. When there was a problem, he gave quiet words of discipline where needed, without intruding on anyone's fun. He was just plain good with kids.

So why didn't *he* have a family of his own? The idea of Nathan with a family that didn't include her sent a sharp pang to the region of her heart.

Finally the group pushed off, out into the swifter current. The rafts were four-seaters, each carrying one adult and three kids of various ages, the older ones responsible for looking out for those who were younger. Rachel, who was the odd adult out, Robert and true-to-her-promise Becky Lynn went with Nathan.

This stretch of river was benign enough, the comparatively slow-moving water no more than chest deep at most. Only after a heavy rain could it turn treacherous. The rocks a short distance downstream were the biggest obstacle. To call it white water might be a slight exaggeration. Still, it required skillful navigation. Otherwise the rafts risked being grounded or caught in the churning whirlpools on the upstream side of the rocks. But that was what made the sport exciting and challenging.

The first part of the ride was slow, almost meandering. Rachel tried to relax and enjoy the dazzling pinks and whites of wild azalea and dogwood intermixed with the fresh greens of new foliage along the riverbanks.

Seated directly behind Nathan, she kept being distracted by the play of muscles in his back and shoulders as he maneuvered the raft in the water. The memory of their recent kiss came to mind, sending renewed sensations curling through her. The ease with which he'd been able to fill her body with sensual craving—after so many years—still unsettled her.

The rafters yelled back and forth good-naturedly, telling jokes and pointing out interesting sights along the way. Beside her, Becky Lynn kept up a steady stream of chatter on everything she thought Robert should know about the subject of rafting. He endured her attention with resigned tolerance, and managed to keep from snapping at the girl or brushing her off.

The current began to pick up speed as they approached the rockier stretch, the ride becoming more like a beginner's roller coaster. They experienced a couple of thrills but nothing too nerve-rattling.

Nathan glanced over at Robert. "How d'ya like it so far?"

Robert grinned, the first natural grin she'd seen from him in weeks. "Not bad."

"As good as riding a bike?"

"Maybe," he conceded. "In a few places."

"Next time," Nathan shouted over the increasing rush of water, "we'll have to try something a little more challenging."

Robert sent him a thumbs-up.

About three-quarters of the way through the trip, one of the other rafts got hung up. While keeping theirs in a holding pattern with the oars, Nathan waited to see how it fared. Getting stuck was more nuisance than danger, but everyone was aware that certain whirlpools could hold a raft hostage until someone was forced to get into the mountain-chilled water and free it. It quickly became evident that this was going to be one of those times.

Nathan guided their raft onto a flat, low-lying rock.

"Want some help?" Rachel asked, climbing onto the warm rocks so she could anchor the raft and keep it from being swept back into the current. Becky Lynn scrambled out after her, but Robert took his time following.

"I'll yell if I need any. This shouldn't be too difficult." Nathan grimaced as he jumped into the cold thigh-high water and waded against the current the few yards to the trapped raft.

"I want to help," announced Becky Lynn. Before

Rachel could stop her, the little girl followed Nathan off the edge of the rock into the water. Although she was tall for her age, what had been thigh-high on Nathan was chest-deep on Becky Lynn. The water might be shallow here, but it wasn't safe to play in outside the raft.

"Becky Lynn Adams, you get back here this instant," Rachel ordered, sliding into the cold swirling water and holding out a hand to the child.

Becky Lynn hesitated, turned to start back toward Rachel, then stopped abruptly. "My foot's stuck!" she cried, struggling to work it free while keeping her balance.

"Sit tight," Nathan called as he maneuvered the other raft free of the whirlpool and into the flowing water. "I'll be right there."

Almost before the words left Nathan's mouth, Robert was in the water, too. Churning sand and bubbles made it impossible to see beneath the surface. Sinking to his knees beside Becky Lynn, he used his hands to fish around to discover what was trapping her foot. "Her foot's wedged between a couple of rocks," he called to Nathan.

Becky Lynn whimpered slightly, but it was clear she was fighting to keep up a brave front.

Robert patted her shoulder awkwardly. "It'll be okay."

Nathan was beside him in seconds. After several frantic minutes, they worked the little girl's foot free and got her back to the rocks. Her sneaker had protected her foot from the worst of it, but all the yanking and prying had bruised her ankle, if not sprained it.

When everyone was back in the raft, a much-subdued

Becky Lynn sat close beside Robert for the remainder of the trip.

Rachel noted that her brother didn't object.

The pickup point was little more than an eyebrow of low-lying sand that gently sloped into the river, furnishing an ideal spot to beach rafts, kayaks and canoes. This was one time Nathan was glad to reach the end of the trip downstream. Not only because of his concern for Becky Lynn's injured foot, but because he'd had all the close proximity to Rachel he could take.

Even with all the confusion, he'd been aware of her eyes on him, analyzing, questioning. She'd always been the only woman capable of challenging his self-control. Not that there had been that many women. But during the darkest period in his life, right after Matthew's death and before he'd found his street ministry, he'd tried to find a substitute. He'd tried...and he'd failed. With effort he shook off those thoughts.

The rafts had to be carried about a dozen yards inland to the gravel parking area where the vans waited. Nathan noticed several motorcycles on the opposite side of the lot, also waiting. The bikers appeared to be in their late teens or early twenties...and looking for trouble.

"Help Becky Lynn, will you?" Nathan said to Robert.

Robert tensed when he spotted the bikers, but he followed Nathan's instructions and crouched beside the girl. "Hop on my back," Robert told her, "and I'll carry you to the van."

A look of surprise, then pleasure brightened Becky Lynn's face. "Thank you," she said and gingerly climbed on.

As Robert started toward the van, the group of bikers began hooting. "Hey, Holcomb, can't you get a chick your own age?"

A muscle worked in Robert's jaw, but he said nothing and kept walking toward the waiting vans.

After telling the others to get the rafts loaded, Nathan leisurely headed in the direction of the bikers. He stopped a yard or so in front of them. From a distance they hadn't looked promising. Close up didn't improve them much. The only positive was that he was certain none of them was Gus Anderson, the leader the sheriff had told him about. They might be little more than kids, but they could still cause trouble. A sick feeling knotted his gut. Damn. He didn't want this. Not here. Not now.

Not in front of Rachel.

Without showing a flicker of concern that there were five of them confronting him, Nathan spoke to the bikers, keeping his voice low. "Don't you have something better to do than heckle folks who're minding their own business?"

One of the bikers spat on the ground and said, "Nah."

The others snickered.

Nathan stared straight into the hostile eyes of the biker who'd spoken, then slowly, deliberately, took one step toward him. "Well, I'll be happy to suggest a couple of useful things you could do."

Something shifted in the kid's eyes. A shadow of doubt. "You must be the preacher man."

"Never was much on preaching." Nathan took another step forward. "But I do believe in telling it like it is. Or showing, if it's necessary."

The spokesman for the group grunted, but this time

he took a step back. "You sure don't talk 'n' act like no preacher I ever met."

Nathan sent him a feral grin. "Have you met many?"

He shrugged. "A few. But you're not like any of 'em," he repeated.

"I'll take that as a compliment," Nathan said. "Now that we've established that I'm different, why don't all of you go on about your business and leave these folks to do the same?"

"Come on, Billy," said another biker. "Let's get outta here."

The spokesman stared at Nathan a moment longer, as if trying to see behind his mask. He must not have liked what he saw. "You're right," he said to the others. "This ain't no fun. Let's go."

Nathan released a sharp breath. He'd been lucky this time. But he knew that eventually this group of kids would have to be dealt with.

The adults converged on Nathan as soon as the bikers had ridden off. But Rachel hung back, taking time to collect herself. She'd watched Nathan take that same stance before. She'd also seen the results. Today had been no different. But still it had terrified her.

"How'd you get them to leave?" Dorthea Wickersham asked in awe.

"We've tried to run them off in the past," Dorthea's sister Penelope added, "but it's usually us who have to go."

Nathan seemed to choose his words carefully. "I think they got bored and wanted to find some other form of entertainment."

"Well, what I want to know is what can be done about this riffraff," someone else chimed in.

"We've got to find a way to fight these people," another said. "More 'n' more of 'em are moving in."

Paul McDaniel, who'd driven Nathan's van to the pickup point, joined the group. He'd arrived in time to hear most of the discussion. "Maybe Nathan has some ideas about what we can do."

"That's right!" someone else added. "He's been working up in Washington with troubled kids."

Rachel saw the muscles at Nathan's jaw tighten. "I'm not going to be in town that long."

"But you could help us while you're here."

"I'm the wrong person for the job," he said.

"How can you be the wrong person?" Penelope said. "You've been working with kids like these, and you're a minister. I can't think of anyone better for the job."

Nathan began loading supplies into his van. "I'm not planning on being a minister much longer."

A shocked silence fell over the group, then murmurs, followed by everyone talking at once.

"But you can't do that," one said.

"This is your hometown," added another.

"Your father's fondest wish was that you'd come back here and take over his church," said a third. "No offense, Reverend McDaniel."

Paul nodded in agreement and said, "None taken."

Nathan smiled a little bleakly. "I think my father had *Matthew* in mind to be minister here."

"Oh, fiddle-faddle," Penelope said, effectively dismissing all their arguments. "As long as you're already here, what's to keep you from helping us out with this?"

Rachel knew by the deliberate manner in which he was loading the van that Nathan didn't want to get into this discussion. But the others didn't seem to notice.

Edgar Hutchins, who was of undetermined age and a dedicated church member, ambled over to Nathan. Rachel knew the older man believed that the secret to staying young was being a part of young people's lives, so he was a standard fixture at these outings.

"I ain't had your schooling," he began, "but I've been around and seen a lot of life. You know what you should do, boy. You've worked in them ghettoes and know what's what when it comes to handling problems bigger 'n this one. Your pa would expect you to do what's right." He patted Nathan on the shoulder with a weathered hand. "You know what's right, son."

Nathan closed his eyes in what seemed to be resignation. "I make no promises," he finally said. "But I'll do what I can."

The resulting praise and gratitude were accepted stoically. Finally Nathan slammed shut the back door of the van. "Now, I believe there's food waiting for everyone back at the church."

Everyone shouted their agreement and piled into the vans.

The ride back to the church was quiet. Becky Lynn had been sent on ahead to have her foot checked over by a doctor. Robert sat in the back seat in brooding silence.

When they reached the church, Nathan pulled around to the back but left the motor idling. Robert immediately opened the door, but before he could get out Nathan put his hand on the boy's shoulder to stop him.

Robert looked at Nathan questioningly.

"What you did for Becky Lynn today," Nathan said quietly, "now *that* was cool."

"Yeah, right." Robert shook off Nathan's hand and bolted from the van.

"That was a nice thing to say to him," Rachel said after a moment. "Thank you."

"Just telling it like it is," he said, sending her a crooked smile.

She gestured toward the ignition keys. "Aren't you going to come in and eat?"

He looked at her for a long, lingering moment. "No, I don't think so."

The amount of disappointment she felt surprised her. By now she should expect this from him. She got out of the van, closed the door, then looked at him through the open window.

"You know, I was thinking," she said, something telling her she would regret what she was about to say. "If you're going to leave the ministry anyway, why not stay in Thunder Ridge? You have to live somewhere. That is—" she paused "—unless you're still running."

Something flashed in Nathan's eyes, but he didn't answer, simply put the van in gear and drove away.

Rachel watched until he was out of sight. Suddenly she realized she was in deep trouble. She was in danger of losing her heart to Nathan all over again.

Chapter Ten

Unless you're still running.

Rachel's last words echoed inside his head as Nathan drove away. She was right. He was still running. He had no desire to confront what he'd given up, no desire to risk reopening that wound. As he left the church parking lot, the last image he caught in his rearview mirror was of Rachel standing where he'd left her.

He needed to put distance between them. Except for the encounter with the bikers, today had been unexpectedly enjoyable. And that made him uneasy. He hadn't yet adjusted to the fact that Rachel still had the power to turn his world upside down. Today he'd discovered that even in a group of noisy people she got to him.

He'd already made one critical mistake last week. He'd kissed her. It had been a tormenting reminder of what he'd denied them both years ago.

Would things have turned out differently, he wondered for the umpteenth time, if he'd ignored all the rational reasons not to take her with him when he'd left to join his brother halfway around the world? She'd wanted to go. But to his mind, it had been out of the question.

She'd been barely twenty and in nursing school, with an urgent commitment to get her eight-year-old brother out of foster care. Until she'd come to live with his family, her life had held few victories. He'd loved her too much not to give her the chance to fulfill her dreams—something she couldn't accomplish following him to a third-world country. He'd tried to explain that to her.

But his explanations had led to something much more elemental. He'd ended up wanting her so badly he'd ached with it. It had taken every ounce of willpower he possessed to keep from making love to her under that hot August sun. Rachel, in her innocence, had been convinced his principles had stopped him.

But it had been self-preservation, not scruples, that had given him the strength necessary to pull away. The simple truth was that he couldn't have made love to her, intimately known her sweetness, then left her behind.

In a dark corner of his heart, he'd always feared that she'd fallen in love with an unrealistic ideal, rather than the man he really was. Even so, he'd intended to return for her after completing his missionary assignment.

But Matthew's brutal death had ripped apart his life, his plans.

Now there was little left inside him except emptiness and a guilt that threatened to consume him. That wasn't enough to offer a woman like Rachel. She deserved a man who was whole. Most of all, she deserved a man who wasn't a fraud.

But God help him, if he had to be alone with her again. He didn't think he could be as noble the next time.

Rachel shifted in bed, trying to find a position that would allow her to drop off to sleep. But it eluded her. She couldn't clear her mind.

Nathan was leaving the ministry.

He was leaving Thunder Ridge.

And she was falling in love with him for the second time.

Rolling from her stomach to her back, she stared up at the shadowy ceiling. She'd sworn she wouldn't make that mistake again. Hadn't she learned anything the first time?

Nathan Garner had been her best friend. She'd fallen in love with his strength, understanding, perception, goodness. She'd entrusted her hopes and dreams to him.

And he'd failed her.

It had been the most painful lesson of her life.

No, she rationalized, she couldn't be falling in love with him again. Today had simply reminded her of their youth, when their feelings for each other had been honest and open. Before things had become complicated, before fate had stepped in to change everything.

Four years older than she, Nathan had left for college a year after she'd come to live with the Garners. Then he'd entered the seminary. But during his infrequent visits home, their friendship had grown and deepened into a love that she'd been certain would last a lifetime.

Her thoughts kept drifting back to that hot August afternoon years ago. It had marked the beginning of the end. Nathan had come to her, saying he wanted to talk to her someplace where they wouldn't be disturbed. He'd been so serious, more serious than she'd ever seen him. The ride to their secluded spot near the falls had been unusually quiet, while foreboding had gnawed at the pit of her stomach....

To escape the unrelenting heat, they left the car for the inviting shade of an ancient oak that clung precariously to the riverbank. They sat propped against its weathered trunk, close together but not touching. The refreshing sound of rushing water held the promise of relief, but Nathan's uneasy silence told her that he had something more important on his mind than cooling off.

Finally he reached for her hand, the strength of his grip communicating his agitation. "It's taken a lot of thinking," he said, "but I've decided to join Matthew on his missionary assignment."

Apprehension curled through her. Nathan's older brother had been assigned to a country so obscure she'd had to look it up in an atlas to locate it. It was a politically unstable third-world nation where the human suffering was equaled only by the danger to those trying to help.

She knew Nathan had been wrestling with this decision for some time. Knew that he felt a deep-seated responsibility to look out for his older, though weaker, brother. Still, she hadn't expected him to make the decision without discussing it with her. She took a fortifying breath. "When do you leave?"

"Tomorrow."

She nodded rather than spoke. From his remote expression she knew she wasn't going to change his mind.

What was there left to say? Instead, she struggled to hang on to her composure.

He stared out at the churning water for long moments before continuing. "You know I want us to be married."

"Now?" she asked, managing—just barely—to control her elation, to keep her voice even. "Before you leave?"

Turning onto his side, he braced himself on one elbow and looked at her. His expression raw, he reached over and gently touched her cheek. "I wish..." He shook his head as if to banish the thought. "Not until I've finished this assignment."

Apprehension became a nameless fear that she was about to lose the most precious thing in her life. "But why wait?" she asked, not caring that she was pleading. "I want to be with you. It doesn't matter where."

He closed his eyes briefly, then opened them to search hers. "What about nursing school?"

True, that had been one of her dreams. She was about to start her third year. But suddenly it didn't seem all that important—not if it meant being thousands of miles away from Nathan. She turned so she could see his eyes, try to read his thoughts, gauge his feelings.

"Your assignment won't last forever. I can finish school when we get back."

"And Robert?" His half smile contained such yearning, she felt her heart crack. "What about him?"

That stopped her. In her excitement she'd momentarily forgotten about her brother, and her dream of making a home for them. "But couldn't we...?"

He was shaking his head before she finished the thought. "You know they'll never give you custody if you're living in some out-of-the-way country halfway around the world.''

Defeated, she leaned over and pressed her face against his shoulder, inhaling the familiar scent of him. This was the man who'd first offered her friendship, then stolen her heart. She drew comfort from his nearness, his strength, acknowledging that he was right even as she searched for an alternative.

He coaxed her head up. ''Look at me,'' he ordered softly. ''I promise you, our time will come.''

But not now. It was such a bleak thought she made no attempt to stop the tears.

His eyes filled with bone-deep longing, and he pulled her to him. For several moments they simply held on to each other. But they couldn't ignore the urgent need to be closer, to capture what fate seemed intent on taking from them.

Nathan's mouth sought hers. At first his kiss was gentle, making silent promises. But it quickly grew more demanding—asking unvoiced questions. It had always been Nathan and his formidable self-control that had held them in check. She prayed this time maybe...

There was a new dimension to the kiss that seemed to mirror the poignancy of their looming separation. If his leaving was inevitable, Rachel thought as desperation began to edge out reason, then she wanted more. If she couldn't go with him, she wanted something she could hold close during the long wait ahead.

She put her heart and soul into the kiss, demanding a commitment of their bodies if not a commitment before God and family and friends. And he seemed as eager as she, his mouth growing hungrier. His hands moved over her body as if he were imprinting the feel of her on his memory. When their clothing became an intolerable barrier, he stripped off both their shirts.

Groaning his anguish, his desperation matching hers, he shifted her beneath him. Impatiently he pushed aside her bra, freed her breast and covered it with his mouth.

The jolt of erotic pleasure was so intense it almost overpowered her senses. Instinctively she pressed closer, unwilling to miss a single sensual nuance, trying to communicate the emotions flooding her.

"Honey, you're so..." He moved so he could work his hands inside the waistband of her shorts to grip her buttocks and hold her tightly against him.

She ran her hands over the smooth, sun-warmed skin of his back, until the waistband of his jeans stopped her. While a lucid corner of her brain told her she should be shocked by her actions, she fumbled with the button at the top of his fly.

With a guttural sound of agony, he rolled to his back and grabbed her hands, holding them against his taut stomach. "Don't..." he panted, resting his forehead against hers. "Sweetheart, we gotta stop."

"Please," she whispered, unashamed that she was begging. "At least give us this—"

As if he couldn't bear to hear her plea, he pulled her down on top of him and silenced her with another kiss. Tears of frustration and yearning trickled down her cheeks to merge with the kiss. Suddenly he bolted upright, dragging her with him.

"We...I..." he said between deep, shuddering breaths, "can't do this...."

Rachel jerked awake—and back to the present—her body still humming, slick with arousal. The faint light coming through the bedroom window told her it was almost dawn. She ran shaking hands through her perspiration-soaked hair. They'd come so close, she thought in frustration and longing and despair.

But he had stopped. That he could have denied them that one binding act should have told her clearer than words that he couldn't possibly have loved her as she loved him.

Perhaps he'd never loved her at all. Perhaps he'd simply thought of her as an obligation.

Pushing herself upright, she leaned back against the pillows. Who was she trying to fool? It wasn't that she was in danger of falling *in* love with Nathan Garner again. Truth was, she'd never fallen *out of* love with him to begin with. She gave a soundless laugh. That would certainly explain why, in all their years apart, she'd never found another man who could come close to touching her emotions as Nathan had.

When he'd first returned to Thunder Ridge, she'd decided that he no longer cared about much of anything. But yesterday, she'd sensed his pain, sensed something deep inside that troubled him.

Years ago she'd thought she'd understood Nathan. Now she realized she'd been mistaken. She'd allowed him to walk out of her life without ever having gotten to the bottom of what made him tick.

Then, she'd been up against impossible odds, a situation she couldn't fight—his duty, her duty, their responsibilities. She'd been helpless to fight for Nathan, for their love.

She'd never gotten over the fact that he'd deserted her just as so many others in her life had done. Could she learn to let go, to trust him again? This time, there was nothing to stop her from fighting for what she wanted.

Nothing but herself.

No, this time she wouldn't make the same mistake. This time, she intended to get to the bottom of whatever was troubling him. For however much longer he remained in Thunder Ridge, she intended to pursue Nathan. And somehow she'd discover his secret.

Chapter Eleven

Rachel leaned back from her desk, stretching out the kinks in her shoulders and neck, surveying the stack of patient charts still left to fill in. She'd been fortunate to find an opening with Dr. Maggie Harper. Jobs for nurse-midwives were tough to come by in a small town, but Rachel had returned to Thunder Ridge just about the time Maggie had decided to cut back on her OB-GYN practice. She'd been delighted to have someone take over part of the load.

Eyeing the waiting charts, Rachel tried to dredge up enough energy to finish them. Normally she didn't mind the paperwork. It was just that this had been an unusually busy day—after several unusually restless nights haunted by erotic dreams of Nathan.

Terry Michaels opened the office door and poked her head inside, saving Rachel from having to dwell on the reason for her lack of sleep. "Ready for your last patient?"

Looking up from the clutter in front of her, Rachel sent her assistant a weary smile. "Since nine o'clock this morning."

Terry grinned. "I'm with you." She walked over to Rachel and dropped another chart on her desk. "Recognize who this is?"

Rachel scanned the name on the chart. Valerie Anderson. It rang a distant bell, but she couldn't quite place it.

"You tell me. You're the one who keeps up with the latest gossip."

Eager to share, Terry lowered her voice to a conspiratorial level. "Her brother's supposed to be the guy who's stirring up all the trouble with the motorcycle crowd."

Rachel studied the chart a little closer. Just what she needed—a patient who was related to the very person she wanted to keep Robert away from. Unfortunately, such was small-town life. "I wonder if Nathan's aware that Gus Anderson has a sister?" she muttered to herself.

"Nathan Garner? Isn't he simply the sexiest minister you've ever met?" Terry asked dreamily.

Her thoughts exactly, but Rachel didn't voice her opinion.

"I hear he's going to handle the problem."

"What problem?" She was having difficulty keeping up with her assistant's somewhat convoluted conversation.

Terry sent her an exasperated look such as a teacher would a daydreaming pupil. "The motorcycle gang."

"Ah," Rachel said dryly, recalling Nathan's reluc-

tance when the church group made that same suggestion. "Someone might want to check with him on that."

"What do you mean?"

"He's not going to be in town much longer."

"That's not what I heard."

That was another thing about small towns—there
were few secrets. "Haven't you learned anything about
rumors?" Rachel mocked good-naturedly. "What gets
passed around as fact doesn't necessarily resemble
truth."

Terry poked her tongue in her cheek. "I hear you've
been seeing a lot of him lately. Maybe I should just ask
you about his plans."

Rachel knew his plans. And they didn't include anyone or anything long-term in Thunder Ridge. She sent
Terry what she hoped was a quelling look. "Maybe you
should send in our last patient, or we'll never get out
of here. Oh, and if Robert shows up before I'm finished,
tell him I shouldn't be too much longer."

"Will do," Terry said, still grinning, and scooted out
the door.

Moments later a *very* pregnant small-boned woman
slipped into the chair across the desk from Rachel. She
estimated the mom-to-be had to be close to eight
months along.

"Hi, Valerie. I'm Rachel Holcomb."

"Hello." The woman spoke in a quiet, almost timid
voice.

Not exactly the demeanor Rachel would have expected from the sister of an alleged gang leader, not
that there was any reason why she should know what
to expect. According to the chart, Valerie was twenty-
four, though she appeared younger. "When was the last

time you were seen by a doctor?'' Rachel began, easing into the exam.

Valerie sat up a little straighter, clutching her hands together in her lap. ''It was before we moved up here.''

''You and your husband?'' Rachel made notes as they talked, hoping to get her to relax.

''Just my brother and me.'' A flush spread across her face. ''I...don't have a husband.''

Rachel nodded. It wasn't her place to be judgmental. Her goal was to help bring the healthiest baby possible into this world. ''Can you give me the date of your last exam?''

''I don't remember exactly. A couple of months ago.''

Masking her concern with an encouraging smile, Rachel began taking her patient's medical history. Valerie answered each question in great detail. By the last one, it was clear that she was as anxious for the well-being of her baby as Rachel.

''Any pains or other complaints?'' Rachel asked, finishing up.

A twinkle entered Valerie's eyes, and she smiled shyly. ''Just the ones you'd expect from someone carrying around a passenger almost as big as she is.''

Rachel chuckled, warming to the woman's subtle sense of humor. ''Well, let's take a look and see how you're both doing.''

Nodding, Valerie followed her into the examining room.

The routine exam didn't take long. When they were back in her office, Rachel said, ''Everything looks fine. But you need to come back next week so Dr. Harper can run a couple of tests.''

A slight frown marred the younger woman's features. "I'll see if my brother can bring me."

"Next week, Valerie," Rachel told her firmly, removing the sting with a smile. "This isn't optional."

"I'll tell him," she promised, but her expression conveyed uncertainty.

"Is he picking you up today?"

"Yes."

"Good." Rachel made a mental note to tell him herself when he arrived. Then she sent Valerie along with a plastic cup to the restroom.

Thirty minutes later, Rachel stepped outside the door of the clinic and scanned the parking lot for Robert. She spotted him, standing beside her car, along with another young man she didn't recall having seen before.

"Robert," she called, starting toward him. "Is everything okay?"

"Yeah," Robert said quickly. "Everything's cool."

Rachel approached the two slowly, noticing that Robert quickly moved out of reach of the older youth who looked to be in his late teens or early twenties. Several inches taller than her brother, he had well-developed arms that suggested he spent a good share of his time working out. Rigorously.

The biker leather he had on lacked style, giving him a trashy appearance. Interesting, she mused, how similar clothing looked different, depending on who wore it. A mental image of Nathan in the same form-fitting outfit filled her mind, catching her off guard. On him, it was just plain...sexy. An unexpected sensual tingle curled through her.

By the time she reached her brother and the newcomer, she'd managed to get her thoughts back on track.

Stopping in front of them, her gaze moved to Robert. "Aren't you going to introduce us?"

He complied, but with obvious reluctance.

So this was Gus Anderson, Rachel thought after the terse introductions were completed. The person responsible for stirring up so much trouble in such a short time. Though it hadn't been confirmed, she suspected he'd had something to do with Robert's recent trip to the hospital. A protective fury threatened to override her common sense.

"I'd hoped to get a chance to speak with you," she said, managing to keep her voice pleasant.

He slouched lower against her car, his expression sullen. "What about?"

"Aren't you Valerie Anderson's brother?"

"Yeah. What of it?"

"I understand she depends on you to get her to and from her doctor appointments."

"So?"

"She has an appointment next week."

Gus shrugged. "I'll try 'n' get her here."

"There's no 'try' to it," Rachel explained carefully, the tenuous control on her temper beginning to slip. "It's important that the doctor sees her."

He gave her a bored look. "She sees the doctor." He nodded toward the clinic. "She's in there right now, ain't she?"

"For the sake of your sister and her baby, it has to be more often than every couple of months."

Gus straightened away from the car to tower over her. "Listen, chick," he said, a sneer contorting his face, "get off my case."

Beginning to understand why her brother had moved

out of this guy's reach, Rachel took an involuntary step back, then held her ground.

Robert, who'd remained silent up to this point, now came to her defense. "Hey, man, don't talk to my sister like—"

"Please, Robert," she snapped, cutting him off, "let me handle this." She caught her brother's stricken look out of the corner of her eye and immediately regretted her words.

Robert quickly masked his reaction with a display of bravado, jamming his hands into his jeans pockets. "Fine," he snarled as he stalked off. "I'm outta here."

Realizing she'd handled the situation poorly, Rachel's first instinct was to go after him. But she needed to finish her business with Gus while fury still gave her the courage.

She forced her attention back to the biker. "No," she said. "I won't get off your case." She took a calming breath. "Someone has to talk sense to you."

His gaze raked her dismissively. "You think you got the guts?"

She was beginning to ask herself the same question. She'd like nothing better than to rail at him for what he'd done to Robert, what he was doing to the community. But that would have to wait until another time. Right now it would be wiser to keep to the original subject, she acknowledged, before things got completely out of hand. She folded her arms protectively across her chest and decided to try to make him see reason.

"Look, all I'm interested in here is Valerie and her baby," she said. "If you care anything at all for your sister, you'll get her to the clinic next week."

Hostility, along with another emotion, flashed in his

eyes. "Keep outta our business," he said, his tone low, almost threatening.

Rachel wouldn't allow herself to back down. "Your sister *is* my business. I'm the person who's supposed to deliver her baby."

He looked at her disbelievingly. "You a doctor?"

"No," she said. "I'm a nurse-midwife."

"Then stay away from my sister. If she's gotta see a doc," he said, jabbing a finger against her shoulder, "it better be a real one."

Realizing she was about to lose control of the situation, she tamped down on her rising apprehension. She was definitely going to make a point of asking Nathan his secret for handling troublemakers so effectively, the next time she saw him.

Chapter Twelve

Nathan drove slowly down the narrow side street. He hadn't been to this part of town in years. One block off the square, the quiet street was flanked on either side by decades-old homes. They sat in neatly kept yards crowded with huge oaks and magnolias and pines. At one time, only families lived here; now a few of the houses had been converted to office space.

This wasn't his usual route home from the small hardware store where he bought the supplies needed for fixing up his house. *His house.* He wasn't certain when he'd started thinking of his parents' place as his. But the more he worked on getting it ready to sell, the more he realized how difficult it was going to be to give it up.

Today he'd picked up a few cans of paint. But an odd restlessness had compelled him to drive past the clinic where Rachel worked. He spotted a sign which read Women's Clinic in front of one of the newer office buildings on this end of the street. As he came abreast of the gravel parking area, he caught sight of Rachel. She was alone—except for a young punk who seemed to be looming over her.

Even from the road he knew their discussion wasn't friendly. The punk had one hand clenched in a fist at his side, the other jabbing a finger at Rachel's shoulder. And Rachel, her arms crossed defensively in front of her, wasn't backing away. Damn, but the woman simply didn't seem to comprehend the meaning of danger.

It was at that moment, as he struggled to contain the explosion of rage and fear, that Nathan admitted just how much she still meant to him. He'd never gotten over her. He'd simply locked away his feelings in the safe dark hole where his heart should have been.

His first instinct was to yank the punk out of Rachel's face, then break his hand. He gritted his teeth. But he wouldn't. Rachel would be appalled. No one had to remind him how much she hated violence. One of the reasons she'd given up her career in Atlanta and moved her brother and herself back to Thunder Ridge was to get away from it.

This had always been his dilemma, Nathan thought ruefully. A minister was supposed to find a peaceful means of settling disputes. But painful experience had taught him that sometimes "peaceful" didn't work. Sometimes it took more than strength of will and silent coercion. Sometimes when all else had failed, it took action.

And he feared that was something Rachel didn't understand.

Clamping down on his anger, he turned into the gravel lot and slowed to a stop beside Rachel. Deciding it wiser for everyone involved if he stayed in the van, he leaned his head out the driver's window and pinned the young punk with a cold stare.

"Afternoon, Rachel," he said, his voice calculatingly casual. "Is there a problem here?"

Before Rachel had a chance to answer, the punk jumped on his bike, revved the engine and took off in a squeal of rubber and flying gravel.

"Wait," she yelled after his retreating figure. "What about Valerie?" But her words were drowned out by the roar of the departing bike. "Damn."

Nathan waited until the bike was out of sight, then brought his attention back to Rachel, studying the frustrated anger heating her cheeks. "Want to tell me what that was all about?"

A stethoscope carelessly draped around her neck, she wore a silky touchable-looking blouse and slacks under her lab coat. She looked professional, yet approachable. A soft breeze ruffled the few strands of auburn hair escaping the long braid that hung halfway down her back.

He'd spent the better part of several sleepless nights thinking about that braid. About undoing it, discovering whether her hair was as long as he remembered. Which was incredibly stupid of him, since he planned to be gone in a very short time. It always left him in a painful state of arousal, and with an empty ache in his heart.

"Gus Anderson," she said succinctly, her troubled eyes finally connecting with his.

It was then that Nathan detected the remnants of fear in them. Fresh anger, and something else, roiled inside him. Needing to touch her, he got out of the van and reached for her arm. "You okay?"

"I'm fine," she said, dismissing his concern.

But he felt the shivers that she failed to hide. Without thought he pulled her into his arms—and felt a deep sense of satisfaction when she didn't resist. It was nothing more than offering comfort, he rationalized. He'd done the same for countless others over the past six years.

But not one of them had affected him like Rachel. He'd never experienced the same powerful emotions as now. The urgency to run his hands over her to assure himself that she was unhurt. The need to kiss her until her fear was replaced by the same sweet passion he'd seen in her eyes days ago. But this was a public parking lot, he reminded himself. So he resigned himself to simply holding her.

"What did he want?"

"You mean other than to be obnoxious?" she asked facetiously against his shoulder. "He was supposed to pick up his sister."

He felt her chest push against his on a frustrated sigh, and he leaned back to look down at her. "You think it's wise to argue with someone like Anderson all alone in a parking lot?"

"Maybe not wise, but definitely necessary. Besides, I wasn't alone...exactly." She glanced around the area, as if suddenly remembering where they were, and pulled out of his arms.

Reluctantly he released her. She put a small amount of distance between them, then ran her hands down the sides of her slacks. The small nervous gesture was the only evidence that she'd been as affected as he by the physical contact.

"Robert's around here somewhere." She frowned up at Nathan questioningly. "Anyway, how'd you know Gus and I were arguing?"

"In my line of work," he said, "you learn to read body language."

She smiled wryly. "Maybe you should give me a few lessons."

Relieved that she'd stopped trembling, he returned her smile. "Maybe I should."

Her spunk had always impressed him, but her total lack of concern for her own safety sent cold chills through him. "Did you even consider the possibility that this guy could be dangerous?"

She tucked a stray strand of hair behind her ear. "This was important. We were discussing a patient, and I was setting him straight on a couple of things."

"First Robert, now a patient," he said, renewed anger and fear building inside him. "Is there anyone you *won't* do reckless things for?"

She sucked in a sharp breath, and he realized he'd spoken more curtly than he'd intended. "Considering the work you do," she said, a slight edge to her voice, "I would think you'd understand."

"What I understand—" he tried to temper his words "—is that you won't do Robert any good by getting yourself injured. Or worse."

The sound of someone coming out of the clinic effectively ended the debate. He resented the interruption. His objective at the moment was to get to the bottom of this tendency Rachel seemed to have for putting herself at risk.

A young woman hesitated at the top of the steps as she surveyed the parking area. Her anxious gaze finally settled on the two of them, and she approached Rachel.

"I thought I heard my brother's bike," the woman said in confusion. "Did he leave without me?"

The woman stopped a few feet away, appearing almost too fragile to be expecting a baby. Nathan found his initial irritation toward the intrusion dissolving. And the meek shall inherit the earth, he thought sardonically. Except he knew that rarely happened without a little help. And this woman obviously needed help.

"I'm sorry, Valerie," Rachel said. "I think I said a few things that...upset him."

Her gaze darted to Nathan then back to Rachel. "Did he say when he'd be back?"

Rachel shook her head. "I'm afraid not."

"Oh." She looked down at her tightly laced fingers.

"Don't worry about it, though," Rachel hastened to assure her. "I'll take you home."

She glanced doubtfully at Rachel's car. "The roads are pretty bad up there. Only a motorcycle or four-wheel-drive can make it. Besides, Gus doesn't like people coming up to the house."

That was one point, Nathan silently acknowledged, where Anderson and he could agree. Unless he was with her, he didn't want Rachel anywhere near Gus Anderson. Taking Valerie Anderson home would have some advantages. While allowing him to keep an eye on Rachel, he could learn a few things about Anderson that might prove useful.

He gave Valerie what he hoped was a winning smile. "Valerie is it?"

Valerie's gaze jerked to his, and she nodded.

"I'm Nathan Garner, a friend of Rachel's." Because Valerie was already jittery, he didn't extend his hand. "Your brother seems to have left you stranded, so it looks like you're going to need another way to get home." He chuckled and glanced down at her rounded tummy. "I think we can safely rule out walking. Since

I have a four-by-four, why don't you let me give you a lift?''

"Oh, no, I couldn't.'' Valerie backed away a couple of paces. "It's a long drive. I'll just sit over there—'' she waved toward the clinic steps "—and wait for Gus. I'm sure he'll be back soon.''

Her faith in her brother was commendable, considering he'd left her here and had yet to return. But working with troubled kids had taught Nathan that sometimes you could find a redeeming feature—if you looked hard enough. The fact that Gus had brought his sister to the clinic in the first place suggested he couldn't be all bad. It gave Nathan a tiny ray of hope that there might be a way to resolve the problem of Gus Anderson.

"He's right, you know,'' Rachel said gently. "The clinic's closing. We can't leave you here by yourself. Besides, I'm not certain I like you riding around on a motorcycle this late in your pregnancy.''

"Oh, dear.'' Another frown pleated Valerie's forehead. "That's the only way Gus can bring me.''

"Well, let's not worry about that right now.'' Rachel put an arm around Valerie's thin shoulders. "Come on,'' she coaxed. "I'll ride along with you. Nathan's a minister. We'll be safe with him.''

"I don't know....'' Valerie said, though obviously she was relenting.

Rachel glanced at Nathan. "I just have to get my things and lock up.'' She began ushering Valerie toward the clinic. "It shouldn't take long.''

"Take your time. I'll go find Robert, then meet you at the van.''

Rachel smiled at him and mouthed a silent thank-you. He prayed everyone's faith in him wasn't misplaced.

* * *

By the time Rachel finished locking up the clinic, there was no sign of Nathan or Robert. While helping a very tired Valerie into the van, Rachel spotted several unopened cans of paint in the back. Emptiness welled within her. They reminded her how temporary Nathan considered his stay in Thunder Ridge. *Until his parents' house was ready to sell.* How much time, she wondered, did that give her?

She glanced around the parking area; Nathan and Robert still hadn't shown up. Leaving Valerie in the van, she followed a hunch that she'd probably find them in the small yard behind the clinic. As she rounded the corner of the building, she caught sight of them through the branches of a large camellia bush.

She was about to call out a greeting, when she heard Robert speak.

"She hates me," he said to Nathan.

Her brother's words froze her to the spot. Robert was hunkered down, his back propped against the brick wall of the building. More than words, his unhappy expression told her how miserable he was.

Nathan crouched beside him, balancing on the balls of his feet. His blue chambray shirt strained against his massive shoulders, and she suddenly realized how often she'd seen him try to put himself on an equal footing with kids, to make his size less intimidating.

"Let me hazard a guess," Nathan said. "We're talking about Rachel?"

"I hate living with her," Robert continued, not bothering to confirm the obvious. "I hate her."

Her brother's bitter words hurt. Though she'd come to expect the frequent clashes with Robert, she'd had no idea he was this unhappy. She'd always imagined that once they became a family again, their relationship would be close. She sighed. Nothing had turned out quite the way she'd expected. Of course, she'd neglected to factor in the problems of dealing with a teenager.

Fighting a pang of sadness, she reminded herself this was what she got for eavesdropping. Yet she couldn't bring herself to walk away.

Nathan didn't try to contradict him. "What happened?"

"Aw, man! She's always making me look like a jerk in front of my friends." He sent a small pebble flying through the air to clatter against a nearby garbage can. "I wish you'd talk to her."

"What'd she do that was so terrible?"

Robert turned to him, his concern undisguised. "Gus *threatened* her! And she was so stupid, she wouldn't let me help. Told me to butt out."

That surprised Rachel. She hadn't realized that Robert had been worried about her. Or that he'd stayed close enough to overhear her confrontation with Gus. How had she failed to consider the fact that her brother might be as concerned for her safety as she was for his?

"Maybe you misunderstood," Nathan suggested mildly. "Are you certain he threatened her?"

She could tell by the tension in Nathan's shoulders that Robert seemed to be confirming what he'd suspected earlier. Nathan had always been protective of her. It had started as soon as she'd come to live with his family. At times she'd resented it. But then, he'd always wanted to help others, regardless the cost to himself. She considered it one of many indications that he was meant to be a minister.

"He told Rachel to stay away from his sister. Told

her he wanted a real doctor to deliver her baby.'' He
paused, then turned his head to stare at Nathan. ''You
don't think he'd hurt her, do you?''

''He won't hurt her.''

Though Rachel couldn't see Nathan's face, she heard
the steel in his voice and shivered. She should let them
know she was there. But if she did, she rationalized, she
might miss something that would help her better understand her brother. Why was it that Nathan was so
good at communicating with him, while she still
couldn't get the knack of it?

''You gonna talk to her?''

''I'll see what I can do,'' Nathan told him. ''Sometimes, brothers and sisters can be a real pain. But usually it's because they love us.''

Robert cut him a quick glance. ''You have a sister?''

''No,'' Nathan said. ''I had an older brother.''

''Had?'' Robert asked. ''Where's he now?''

''He's dead.''

The deep sadness resonating in his voice made her
ache. It was a simple statement of fact, and she was
certain he was waiting for it to sink in. She'd witnessed
how Matthew's death had affected him. He'd been
numb with grief.

She felt another pinch from her conscience for continuing to listen to something so intensely personal, but
again she tried to rationalize it away. Six years ago she
and Nathan had never gotten a chance to talk about it.
Everything had happened too quickly. He'd obviously
been hurting, and she'd been unable to get through to
him. Immediately after the funeral he'd stunned her by
breaking off their engagement.

Then he'd run.

Heartsick, she'd convinced herself that it had been

his grief talking. That once he'd had a chance to heal, he'd contact her. But she'd been wrong. He never had.

At his father's funeral, only months after Matthew's, Nathan had been distant and withdrawn, and pride had kept her from trying to breach his defenses. He'd kept running. From the people who loved him—and, she now confirmed, from himself.

She knew he still was.

After several moments, Robert said, "That's rough."

Nathan nodded in agreement, then reached over and gave Robert's shoulder a squeeze. "Look on the bright side. As long as Rachel's around to argue with, there's always hope you can change her mind."

"Yeah, I guess you're right," Robert conceded, most of his belligerence now gone. "Man, I wish you weren't planning to leave."

Rachel felt tears sting her eyes. Years ago, she'd said something very similar to Nathan. Since then the questions were always there—in the back of her mind, on the tip of her tongue. *Why did you leave? Why did you go away and never come back?*

Why did you turn your back on what we had?

"I'll be around a while longer," Nathan told him and straightened to his feet. "Come on. Your sister's probably waiting for us."

To avoid discovery and give herself time to compose herself, Rachel slipped away to the parking area. She owed her brother an apology.

She owed Nathan even more.

Chapter Thirteen

"It's open," Nathan called in answer to the persistent knocking at the front door. Again dipping his brush into the can of clean white paint, he hoped whoever was there would take the hint and make their visit brief. He was days behind his schedule for getting the house ready to sell. Today he intended to finish painting the kitchen, then start on his father's study. If he didn't get caught up soon, he'd have to consider hiring someone besides Robert to help him.

Yet leaving Thunder Ridge with a clear conscience would be impossible until he knew Robert had his head on straight. He could do that much for Rachel. He knew what her brother meant to her. And he knew intimately the devastation losing a brother could cause. But Robert seemed to be coming around. Now all Nathan had to do was take care of the Gus Anderson problem. And providing he'd taken care of everything else, he would be free to leave.

Wouldn't he?

Light footsteps came to a halt at the kitchen door, but he didn't look up from his task. When he'd finished applying the last paint stroke to the window trim and his visitor still hadn't spoken, he glanced over his shoulder to find the reason for his recent sleepless nights standing in the doorway.

Rachel.

"Hi," she said, and smiled.

His heart gave a chaotic lurch. "This is a pleasant surprise," he said, wondering if she had any idea how inadequate that comment was. To give himself something to do, he set down his brush and grabbed a rag to wipe the paint off his hands.

Her smile grew wider. "Those are the best kind." She walked into the room and gave it a 360 degree sweep. "Looks great," she pronounced when her gaze settled on him again. She strolled across the floor and came to a halt in front of him. "I brought you a gift."

His gaze traveled from her modest emerald green tank top, to white shorts that revealed no more than an appropriate amount of smooth leg, to practical sandals that showed off slender feet. The only thing shocking about her was the shade of pink polish on her toenails. Yet she looked sexier than any of his fantasies—sleeping or waking. He felt heat spread through the lower region of his belly.

"You?" he asked, with what he was sure was a ridiculously hopeful look on his face.

A startled expression crossed hers, but she rallied quickly and smiled. "In a manner of speaking."

"Is it safe to ask what manner we're discussing?"

"I'm here to offer my—" she ran a measuring glance down the length of him, taking in his paint-spattered shirt, ratty shorts and sneakers, then retraced the path to his eyes "—services."

He identified the hint of mischief, while recognizing that this was a side of Rachel he'd never witnessed before. And though his brain knew she was teasing, his libido hadn't taken notice. Even so, he couldn't resist playing along. "Yeah? Are you any good?"

She sent him another provocative smile and moved closer. Now she was within touching distance. "Very," she whispered.

The heat in his belly shot up several degrees. "But I bet you charge more than I can afford."

Because the weather had promised to be hot, he'd left his shirt unbuttoned. She boldly ran the tip of her finger down the length of his bare chest. "I'm willing to negotiate."

"Then by all means," he said, wondering just how far she was going to take this, not to mention just how much his self-control could handle, "show me what you can do."

"I'm here to offer myself—" she grinned, walked over to his abandoned paint brush and picked it up "—as a painter."

He exhaled a sigh, having no difficulty feigning disappointment. "Too bad."

"You're not interested?" Her hazel eyes still sparkled with laughter.

"I didn't say that." He sent her a lopsided grin. "I was just wondering, why you? Isn't this supposed to be Robert's job."

"He's got exams this week. And since we're responsible for taking up so much of your time, I decided to offer my help until he's free.''

Funny, only moments ago he'd been telling himself he needed more help. But somehow he didn't like hearing it from Rachel. ''You trying to get rid of me?''

''No,'' she said, suddenly serious. ''I'm trying to say thank you.''

''For what?''

''For helping Robert. For taking Valerie home.'' She pinned him with clear hazel eyes. ''For being you.''

Her sincerity got to him. But he didn't want her gratitude. Everything he'd done was really for himself. To keep her safe, unchanged. She looked so clean, untouched, standing there, representing all that had been good in his life, the last vestiges of a simpler past. She was everything he'd ever wanted in a woman, lover, wife. He wanted....

Truth was, he was afraid to name what he wanted.

''Well,'' she said, after several long moments of silence, ''let's see what you've done with the place.''

She left the kitchen, and he followed her to the living room. It had taken him several nights of hard work, sometimes into the wee hours, to complete the project. He'd used it as a means of relieving some of his frustration. Letting his gaze travel around the room, he tried to see it as she did. The massive stone fireplace and mantel had been scrubbed until they looked almost new. The oak paneling and floor had been waxed and buffed to a rich patina. He was pleased with the results.

He glanced at Rachel to find her studying him. ''It's beautiful,'' she said, running her hand over one of the doors he'd meticulously stripped, sanded and restained.

''Thanks. I enjoyed working on it.''

''I can tell.'' She scanned the room and chuckled. ''I

remember the first time I saw this room. It seemed enormous.''

''I remember the first time I saw you in it.'' He walked over to the old sofa and sat down, stretching his legs out in front of him. ''You were sitting right here, trying not to look terrified.''

''Was it that obvious?''

''Maybe not to everyone, but it was to me. That and a few other things.''

''Yeah?'' She came over to sit within arm's reach of him on the sofa. ''Like what?''

''Like you needed a friend.'' His father had told the family that both of Rachel's parents were dead, and that her baby brother had been placed in another foster home. Nathan had sensed how lost she'd felt, like an outsider, an intruder. He'd been able to identify with her, having always felt much the same, even in his own home.

A reminiscent smile curved her mouth. ''Did I ever thank you for taking me under your wing, so to speak? You made those first few days a little less frightening.''

''Maybe I had an ulterior motive.'' To give himself an excuse to touch her, he reached over and tucked a strand of hair behind her ear.

''Now this sounds interesting,'' she said, her eyes dancing again.

Realizing they were heading into dangerous territory, he withdrew his hand and came to his feet. ''Didn't you tell me you were here to help me paint?'' he said, changing the subject.

''No fair,'' she said. ''Not until you explain what you meant by ulterior motive.''

He studied her for several moments, debating with himself before answering. She was watching him now as she had all those years ago, with hazel eyes much too warm for her own good. Or his.

"Maybe I wanted you to like me." He laughed in self-deprecation. "Another thing I noticed about you right away was how you made me feel. Things that a seventeen-year-old guy definitely shouldn't be feeling for a thirteen-year-old girl who was going to be living under the same roof."

By her stunned expression he knew he'd surprised her.

Figuring he'd repaid her for her earlier performance, he smiled wickedly. "Now are we ready to paint?"

Jumping to her feet, she grinned right back. "Sounds like a plan to me," she said affably, then beat him down the hall to the kitchen.

As they worked, Nathan kept eyeing her. Other than to ask a question now and then pertaining to the task at hand, she hadn't said much since they'd begun painting. She seemed contemplative, and he wondered what was going on inside that beautiful head of hers.

They fell into a comfortable routine and by noon had finished the kitchen. Deciding to take a break before starting on the study, they fixed sandwiches, opened cans of soda and ate at the old kitchen table that had been in his family since he was a boy.

For the first time in longer than he cared to remember, Nathan realized he was experiencing something close to contentment. Feeling the familiar longing that had taken him years to subdue, he tried to dismiss it. He'd learned to live with the loneliness. It wasn't prudent to admit that he'd missed Rachel. Missed the life together they might have had. Missed the love they could have shared.

It scared him. He couldn't afford any emotional entanglements. It had taken him too many painful years to lock away his feelings. He had serious doubts he'd have the strength to do it again.

It was after they'd finished putting away the painting supplies for the day that Rachel spotted the small box on the corner of the desk where he'd left it several days ago.

"I remember this," she said, picking up the old metal box. "It belonged to your father." Shaking it gently, she heard something thump against its sides. She raised an eyebrow in question. "What's in it?"

He stopped what he was doing. Resting his hands loosely on his hips, he watched her. "Don't know. I haven't found the key."

She turned the box over several times, frowning. "Wait a minute. I remember your mother used to keep a bunch of extra keys on a hook inside the hall closet. Did you check those?"

He shook his head.

She laid the box back on the desk and quickly left the room.

Nathan remained where he was.

Moments later, she returned triumphantly holding a large metal ring containing a dozen or more mismatched keys. "I'll bet it's one of these." She held it out to him.

But instead of taking it from her, he said, "Why don't you do it?"

"You sure?" she asked, studying him again.

"Yeah." For some reason a part of him was reluctant to discover what the box contained.

Rachel flipped through the collection of keys until she came to a likely fit. Sliding it into the lock, she turned it. There was an audible click as the lock opened,

and he felt his stomach roil with a mixture of antici-
pation and apprehension.

When she lifted the lid, they found a cream-colored
envelope inside. Across the front, in his father's careful
handwriting, was written "To my son, Nathan." Nathan
gently picked it up and turned it over, noting that it was
sealed.

"Aren't you going to open it?" she asked softly.

He couldn't imagine why his father would have written to him. If it was important, why had Nathan never
received it? The knot in his stomach expanded.

"Not right now." He put the envelope back inside
the box and closed it.

Rachel studied him a few seconds longer, unasked
questions intensifying the gold in her hazel eyes. "Well,
I need to get back to the house. Robert will be home
soon."

Nathan nodded and started walking her down the hall.
"I appreciate everything you did today."

"You're welcome. Robert will be available by the
end of the week to help again."

"Speaking of Robert…" He paused.

"Yes?"

"He asked me to have a word with you."

She stopped when they reached the front door. "Oh?
About what?"

"Now, I'll admit I'm as much in the dark as the next
person when it comes to the workings of a teenager's
mind," he began wryly. "But I do know an adolescent
male has, shall we say, a delicate ego. You might want
to watch what you say to Robert when he's around his
'friends'…even the less savory ones."

She grimaced. "We're talking about the little incident in the clinic parking lot with Gus?"

He nodded.

"I know I embarrassed Robert. And I've apologized." She rubbed her arms, and Nathan thought he caught a trace of sadness in the smile she sent him. "But I don't think he's forgiven me yet."

"Give him time. He'll come around."

"Thanks for the advice." She fished her car keys out of her shorts pocket, then glanced around her. "You've certainly put an awful lot of work into a house you plan to get rid of."

Her observation was something he didn't want to examine too closely. He shrugged. "Like I said, I enjoy the work."

Rachel looked up at Nathan and sensed his deep yearning. He understood other people so well, but when it came to his own emotions, he seemed intent on denying them. Just how difficult was it going to be to discover the secrets he was hiding? To get him to open up and share them with her?

And once he had, how much more painful was it going to be this time for her to let him go?

She laid her hand against his slightly roughened jaw. The muscle there jumped, and his eyes darkened. Without thinking she lifted her mouth and touched it to his.

For a brief moment he remained motionless, allowing her to kiss him. But she sensed his struggle against tightly leashed emotions. Then he dragged in a shuddering breath and set her away from him.

"You better go," he said gently, though his voice sounded rusty.

Disappointment skittered through her.

"You know," she said, realizing her voice was equally husky, "sooner or later we all have to confront our ghosts."

Chapter Fourteen

Robert jogged down the tree-lined street that took him from the clinic where Rachel worked to the church where he was supposed to meet Nathan. Rounding the corner about a block from his destination, he spotted Becky Lynn Adams standing in the middle of the sidewalk staring up into the branches of a huge oak tree.

Hoping she hadn't noticed him, he slowed his pace and debated what to do. He wasn't too keen on getting caught up in any more discussions with Becky Lynn. She could talk the ears off a chicken. He considered his options. If he ducked behind the nearest house, he might be able to avoid her. All he'd have to do was cut through a few backyards to get to the church. But something about the way she kept concentrating on that tree stopped him. Resignedly he walked over to her.

"What's up, kid?"

Becky Lynn turned somber brown eyes on him.

Instead of seeing her usual irritatingly happy face, he watched two big tears roll down her cheeks. It gave him a weird feeling in the pit of his stomach. Even when she'd hurt her ankle while they were rafting, she hadn't cried.

"What's the matter?" he asked again.

She scrubbed away the tears. "Up there," she said, pointing.

Robert searched the branches, wondering what he was supposed to be looking for.

"Don't you see her?"

"See who?"

"My kitty."

"Kitty? You're crying 'cause a dumb cat's up a tree?"

"She's not dumb," Becky Lynn defended loyally. "She just can't get down."

"Of course it can," he told her in exasperation. "All cats climb trees." He refused to think of the cat in terms of he or she. If he did, he might begin to care about the thing. Man, wouldn't the guys get a big laugh outta that?

"I didn't say she couldn't climb *up*." She sent him a reproachful look. "I said she couldn't get *down*."

Things went from bad to worse when Robert picked up the rumble of motorcycles in the distance. They were still a few blocks away and moving slow, but he knew once they reached the corner of this street, the guys would spot him. "Look, I can't do anything about this. The cat'll come down when it wants to, okay?"

"But you have to."

"Have to what?"

"Help me," she said plaintively.

With an ear on the approaching bikes and an eye on Becky Lynn, he asked, "Why do I have to?"

"Because you're bigger 'n me."

"Right. And that's why I can't." He'd suffered enough embarrassment in front of the guys recently. He could do without any more.

She looked at him in confusion. "That doesn't make any sense."

Aw geez, he thought, he wasn't going to be able to leave the stupid cat up in the tree—not with Becky Lynn looking at him with those big brown accusing eyes. Maybe if he hurried, he could get it down and be gone by the time the guys showed up. Conceding defeat, he wondered if this was what it was like for his sister when she had to deal with *his* problems. How many times had she been forced to do things she didn't want to…for him?

"Can you keep a secret?" he finally asked.

"Depends."

"Depends? You're supposed to say yes."

"Why?"

It was his turn to shake his head in confusion. "I don't know, you just are."

"But I have to know what the secret is before I know if I can keep it."

Obviously that made perfect sense to the kid. He exhaled a frustrated breath. "Look, if the guys find out about this, I'll never hear the end of it."

"Oh, I see." She smiled up at him. "I won't tell anybody."

Muttering under his breath, he grabbed a low-hanging limb and hoisted himself into the tree. Finding the cat was easy. He simply followed its pitiful mewing until he located it a couple of branches higher, clinging stubbornly to the trunk of the tree.

Getting the silly creature down, however, was another story. It didn't seem to appreciate his attempts at rescue and kept steadily backing away from him. If it backed out much farther on that limb, both of them were in danger of taking a straight shoot to the ground. In desperation, Robert lunged, at last snagging hold of the kitten. Not much bigger than his fist and still terrified, it expressed its indignity by sinking teeth and claws into his hand.

Robert yelped and stuffed the kitten inside his jacket, then shinnied down the tree. As he jumped to the ground, six motorcycles, with Gus leading the pack, cleared the corner and rolled to a stop beside them.

The racket was deafening. Becky Lynn moved closer to Robert, latching onto his arm. The way she huddled against him told him she was frightened.

On a signal from Gus, the bikers silenced all six engines.

"This your new—uh—little friend?" Gus asked Robert, eyeing Becky Lynn with disdain.

Ignoring the sneer, Robert extracted the kitten from his jacket. "Take the cat," he told Becky Lynn, shoving it at her, "and go home."

She carefully took it from him. "Thank you," she said.

Robert noticed that the ungrateful animal immediately settled into her arms and began purring.

"Aw, ain't that sweet?" mocked one of the bikers. "He's got a kitty cat."

Becky Lynn turned on the biker, clutching the kitten to her chest. "It's mine," she told him fiercely.

"You oughta get yourself a dog," another taunted, and the group guffawed.

Without blinking, Robert stared Gus square in the eyes. This time, he wasn't going to allow himself to be intimidated. He sure as heck wasn't going to let anyone intimidate Becky Lynn. Just why, he couldn't say. Robert realized he was making an irrevocable decision, one he'd almost made several days ago when he'd tried to stand up to Gus on Rachel's behalf.

"Tell them to leave her alone," Robert told him. "They're scaring her."

"It's okay." Becky Lynn looked up at Robert, her eyes solemn and full of remorse. "I'm sorry. I didn't mean to get you in trouble with your friends."

"Don't worry about it, kid," Robert told her. "It doesn't matter."

And to his amazement, he knew it was the truth.

Even inside the muffled confines of the church Nathan heard the low rumble of the bikes. He estimated them to be no more than a block away, two at most. It was an unusual sound, coming from the quiet neighborhood that backed up to the church property. Glancing at the antique wall clock in what used to be his father's office, he frowned. Robert should have been here by now.

The reason he'd suggested Robert meet him at the church rather than the clinic, Nathan freely admitted to himself, was because he was a coward, pure and simple. He'd recognized the ploy behind Paul McDaniel's request to drop by the church. Nathan had used the same technique himself enough times when trying to coerce some unwary soul into doing what he wanted. Paul had wanted one more crack at talking him out of giving up the ministry and leaving Thunder Ridge for good, and Nathan hadn't relished the prospect of facing the minister again.

His mouth curved wryly, and he shook his head. He'd figured Robert's arrival would short-circuit Paul's latest campaign. But Nathan could have saved himself the effort. Before Paul had a chance to begin, he'd been called away unexpectedly on other church business.

But the fundamental reason for hiding out in the church had been that Nathan wasn't certain he was ready to face Rachel again. Not after the day they'd spent together. Not after she'd managed somehow to get past the layers of armor he'd forged over the years to protect his heart.

Not after her sweet tentative kiss—a kiss that had almost destroyed him. It had been warm and giving and caring. Restraining himself from making love to her had taken every ounce of self-control he possessed. He had serious doubts he'd be strong enough to say no a second time.

Hearing the rumble of the bikes abruptly cease, Nathan forced his thoughts back to the present. He went to the window and looked out, but he couldn't see beyond the densely wooded area at the back of the parking lot. Instinct told him he'd better check out what was going on.

Something—just what, he wasn't certain—had prompted him to ride the Harley today. Oddly it had been a while since he'd felt the urge to travel down some open highway with only the wind for company. Now he debated whether to take it, or go on foot. He'd learned from experience to use whatever advantages he had at hand. Walking would give him the element of surprise. Riding the Harley would be quicker. It would also make a statement, put him on an equal footing with the other bikers. The bike won.

Moments later, he was riding down the hill behind the church. He spotted Robert, standing protectively beside Becky Lynn at the base of the hill. Six punks, all still straddling their bikes, formed a semicircle around the two. Even without helmets the bikers appeared menacing. Three of them Nathan hadn't seen before. Two others he remembered from the confrontation at the river. Gus Anderson he recognized from their brief encounter a few days ago in the clinic parking lot.

Anger was Nathan's first reaction. He'd never had patience with anyone who would intentionally hurt another living thing, physically or emotionally—particularly someone smaller or weaker. Coming to a stop, he casually positioned his bike between Robert and Becky Lynn and the bikers, then cut the motor.

''Why don't you take Becky Lynn home,'' he suggested to Robert, ''before her kitten gets scared and tries to climb a tree?''

''Right,'' Robert muttered. ''Why didn't somebody think of that sooner?'' He sent Nathan a perturbed look, but started shepherding Becky Lynn away.

Nathan turned his attention to Gus Anderson. ''This is the second time I've caught you harassing someone smaller than yourself.'' He sliced his gaze to include the others. ''Makes me wonder if that's how you and your friends get your kicks.''

Keen interest and obvious intelligence flickered in the depths of the younger man's eyes as he sized Nathan up. ''You sure don't look like a minister,'' he said dismissively.

''Yeah,'' Nathan agreed, not surprised Anderson knew who he was. ''I hear that a lot.'' Though close to himself in build and height, Anderson was younger than he'd first estimated—somewhere around twenty. Being young would make him doubly dangerous and effective. He'd relate more easily to the teenagers he was trying to recruit. "You ever try taking on someone your own size?"

"Hey, man, Robert can take care of himself," Anderson said defensively.

"Maybe. But can you say the same for Becky Lynn? Or Rachel Holcomb?"

Anderson bristled, obviously recognizing the challenge to his authority, as well as his manhood. "You trying to tell me something?"

His eyes now held the blank look of someone who'd lived a rough life and learned to hide his emotions well. Yet Nathan sensed that the emotions were still there, lurking just beneath the surface. Whether that was good or bad remained to be seen.

"Just wondering if you're quite as enthusiastic when it comes to someone who's more evenly matched."

"You wanna find out?"

Nathan didn't blink. "Are you offering?"

Anderson shifted, showing the first sign of unease, and glanced around at the other members of his crew before returning his gaze to Nathan. "Now, I wouldn't wanna be accused of taking advantage of a minister."

The group snickered.

Nathan recognized that Anderson was trying to save face, blow off a possible confrontation that might hold ramifications he hadn't considered. But unlike the incident at the river, this time Nathan couldn't yield. Otherwise the chances of ever discouraging this group would be less than dismal.

He quickly ran through his options. What he'd like

to do was knock some sense into a few heads, but he put that idea on hold. He wouldn't resort to action—not if he could help it. Not with the handful of neighbors, who'd begun straggling out to investigate the ruckus, watching with avid interest. Not with Robert, who'd already returned from seeing Becky Lynn home, standing nearby, studying the situation intently. That left Nathan to come up with an acceptable alternative.

"Fair enough. Let's keep it simple then." He glanced at Gus's bare arms, noting the muscles that could have only been honed by rigorous workouts. "Ever done any arm wrestling?"

Anderson gave Nathan the once-over, seeming to consider the pros and cons carefully. "Yeah, I've done some," he said. "But why should I mess with you? What's in it for me?"

"Do it!" egged one of the bikers Nathan remembered from the incident at the river. "Let's get this dude off our backs."

"I dunno, man," another biker muttered doubtfully. "A minister? Ain't that like tryin' to wrestle with a higher power or somethin'?"

Nathan realized he was treading a fine line. If handled right, this might put an end to Gus Anderson's influence over the town's youth. If not, the whole thing could blow up in Nathan's face.

"If you win," Nathan told him, "I leave you and your friends alone."

"And if I don't?" Anderson asked, but his smile had grown cocky with confidence.

"You have to give me two days a month to explain to the local kids why it's stupid to belong to a gang."

Anderson's smile waned, as if he were searching for the catch. "That's it?"

"That's it." Nathan grinned. "Do we have a deal?"

"Yeah," he said slowly. "I guess so."

Since the church was only a block away, Nathan suggested everyone adjourn there. A couple of the bikers weren't too thrilled about the location, but grudgingly they went along. The other onlookers also followed.

By the time they'd set up a table in the basement of the church, the crowd had grown, with more people steadily trickling in. Nathan sighed. The gossip mill, it seemed, was as efficient as ever. He hoped he hadn't made a grave error in judgment. But he consoled himself with the fact that Anderson and he were close enough in height and weight to make the match fair.

"Y'know, Gus has himself a reputation as an arm wrestler," one of the bikers informed Nathan expansively.

"Does he?" Nathan pulled a chair over to the table and sat down.

"Yeah. I've seen him beat men bigger 'n you."

"So, you know how the game's played?" Nathan asked, ignoring the subtle warning.

"Yeah," the biker said and grinned evilly. "But I wouldn't call it no game."

"Good," Nathan said. "You want to referee?"

The biker looked momentarily taken aback, before grunting his agreement.

Nathan returned his attention to Anderson. "Ready?"

"Yeah." Anderson snagged another chair and sat down across the small table from him.

The newly appointed referee turned to the spectators. "Anybody wanna place a bet?"

He got an elbow in the ribs from a buddy standing next to him. "Not now, man," he whispered, nervously scanning the others. "We're in a church."

''Uh...yeah...right.'' The referee cleared his throat. ''You know the rules?'' he asked Nathan.

If it weren't for the seriousness of the situation, Nathan would have grinned. ''I think I have a fair idea.'' He didn't mention that he'd used arm wrestling on more than one occasion. He'd found it an acceptable means of settling differences among inner-city kids who too often resorted to far more deadly methods.

Placing his bent elbow in the center of the table, Nathan waited for Anderson to follow suit and clasp his right hand with his own. While the referee made certain that the hold was legal with elbows properly aligned, Nathan quickly scanned the crowd of spectators. His gaze jerked to a halt when he encountered Rachel across the room. Their eyes locked for the space of several heartbeats, her troubled expression telling him he didn't want to think about what might be going through her mind right now.

The crowd seemed to hold its collective breath. He forced himself to focus on what he'd committed to do as the referee, giving the signal to begin, released their fisted hands. Anderson threw his weight into it, offsetting Nathan's answering force. Some of the onlookers began to chant.

Nathan had wrestled stronger men and won, but because his reputation was on the line, Anderson would put everything he had into winning. Victory, Nathan knew, depended on his holding steady until Anderson allowed his concentration to lapse. Nathan bided his time, waiting for the slightest hint of a wobble, a weakening in the rigid muscles countering his own. It took less time than he'd anticipated. Anderson committed the cardinal error in competition—he underestimated his opponent.

As soon as he sensed it, Nathan slammed his right arm down, pinning Anderson's to the table. The bikers' stunned silence perfectly matched Anderson's stunned expression. A cheer went up from the neighbors.

For a split second, embarrassment darkened the younger man's face. "Best two outta three," Anderson demanded between gritted teeth.

Nathan sent Rachel a quick glance. She still stood in the same spot she had since she'd entered the room, her usually expressive face now unreadable. Again he wondered what was going on in her head.

He brought his attention back to Anderson. To lose once was embarrassing, to lose twice, Nathan understood too well, would be humiliating. Under cover of the surrounding noise, he asked, "Do you think that's wise? It was a clean match. Why not let it lie?"

Anderson bristled. "You refusing?"

By now the crowd had quieted and was avidly listening. Nathan sighed in resignation. "No. If you're certain it's what you want."

Anderson's eyes glinted with determination. "Damn straight."

"Then let's do it."

As Nathan feared, this time defeat came even quicker.

The gang members registered disbelief at their leader losing a second time. Nathan saw humiliation and fury replace Anderson's earlier embarrassment.

While the neighbors converged on Nathan, pounding him on the back, offering congratulations, the bikers began drifting away.

"Where d'ya think you're going?" Anderson shouted after them.

"Hey, man, this is bigger 'n us."

"I ain't messin' with this."

The other bikers mumbled their agreement as they headed out the door.

"Run then," Anderson sneered. "I don't need any of you."

Nathan sensed the desperation in the younger man. "You can't expect friends to remain loyal," he told him quietly, "when you ask them to back the wrong cause."

"Keep your damned advice. This is your fault." Anderson stood so quickly, his chair toppled backward. "I owe you," he said, stabbing his finger at Nathan's chest, before slamming out of the church.

Nathan didn't have time to dwell on the threat. The neighbors were too intent on congratulating him before leaving to spread this latest bit of gossip. When only a handful of people remained, his eyes sought out Rachel. She stood off to one side, alarm obvious in the rigid way she held herself.

The hollow feeling that had been a part of him for so long seemed to expand.

Chapter Fifteen

Rachel froze where she was, fighting to control her disbelief and the growing apprehension that snaked through her. Gus Anderson had threatened Nathan in front of a roomful of people, and she was savvy enough to realize he would consider it a matter of "honor" to make good on the threat. Yet Nathan appeared unconcerned. Was he so accustomed to living with violence that one threat more or less had little meaning? A small ache began to build in the region of her heart.

Shortly after Robert had left to meet Nathan earlier this afternoon, a patient had brought word of the confrontation near the church involving bikers. Rachel's immediate worry had been whether her brother had run into more trouble. As soon as she could get away from the clinic, she'd left to investigate for herself. Finding Robert among the spectators at the church watching Nathan arm wrestle Gus Anderson had done little to lessen her uneasiness.

Nathan's words to Gus had been reasonable, Rachel recalled, not confrontational. His argument had been logical, convincing. Though she'd never had the opportunity to hear him, she could well imagine that when he delivered a sermon, not a single person in the congregation would fail to listen, or to understand his message. Yet Gus hadn't seemed to. She shivered.

Glancing around the large recreation room, she realized that only the three of them remained. Her brother was helping Nathan stack the table and chairs along the far wall.

"I wish I coulda done what you just did," Robert said to him after a couple of minutes.

Nathan set another chair on the growing stack. "And what's that?"

"Beat Gus. Send him running."

She felt Nathan's gaze settle on her briefly before he responded to Robert. "By the time I arrived on the scene earlier, it looked like you were doing a fair job of holding your own against Anderson and his crew."

"Nah. What I did wasn't cool. It was—" Robert grimaced "—I dunno...wimpy."

"I wouldn't call standing up to Gus Anderson wimpy."

Standing up to Gus Anderson? Her misgiving expanded, forcing her to relinquish her spot on the opposite side of the room. "Does one of you want to tell me what's going on?" she asked, moving closer to them. She worked very hard at keeping her voice neutral, well aware that nothing silenced Robert faster than some sign of what he interpreted as her distressed-sister act.

Robert concentrated on collecting chairs and pretended to ignore her.

To cover her concern, she laid her purse aside, grabbed a chair and scooted it over to Nathan.

Taking it from her, he added it to the stack, before sending Robert an assessing look. But her brother didn't answer. "Robert came to Becky Lynn's rescue today," Nathan finally offered.

"Oh?" She glanced from Robert to Nathan. "What happened?"

When Robert remained mute, Nathan added, "Seems Anderson and his buddies were harassing her."

"I see," she said slowly. The memory of Robert's recent trip to the hospital edged its way into her thoughts, making it difficult to mask her alarm.

Robert's face flushed and he finally spoke up. "It was no big deal. All I did was get her dumb cat down outta the tree," he said, sounding almost defensive. "Gus didn't back off until Nathan showed up."

Her brother had climbed a tree to rescue a cat for a six-year-old child in front of his all-important biker friends. And it was no big deal? She seriously doubted that a week ago he'd have been caught dead sticking up for anyone, certainly not a little girl. But studying him now, she thought she detected a new maturity in him and experienced a jumble of pride and love that tempered her earlier fear. Maybe he'd begun to recognize the danger this group of punks posed not only to himself, but to others in the community.

Nathan put his hand on Robert's shoulder, giving him a gentle shake. "Showing compassion doesn't make you weak or a wimp," he said. "It took more guts to help Becky Lynn, knowing the hassle you'd take from your friends, than if you'd walked away from her, pretending to be 'cool.'"

"Yeah?" Robert's slow smile was lopsided before his forehead creased into a puzzled frown. "Still, cool's cool, y'know?"

"Cool's being true to yourself—no matter what other people think. Hiding your emotions might make you appear strong on the surface. But helping someone weaker than yourself takes real strength."

Robert thought about that for several moments. "I don't think that's how those guys see it. They have to believe you're tough before they'll respect you."

Nathan slowly shook his head from side to side. "You have to respect yourself before you can expect others to respect you."

Rachel sensed her brother struggling to understand something that a few days ago he would have shrugged away. She found it difficult to speak around the lump in her throat. "Nathan's right."

"He is?" Robert's surprise was obvious.

She let go of the chair she'd started to push over to the wall and walked over to him. "I'm very proud of you."

"You are?"

That caused her a moment's pinch of shame. Had she been so absorbed with her concern over who Robert was associating with that she'd failed to make other equally important things clear to him? "Yes, I am," she said and pulled him into a fierce hug.

Robert stood rigid for several moments before she felt his arms awkwardly come around her to return the hug. She leaned back to look up at him. When had he grown so tall? When had he become more man than boy? And how much of this metamorphosis was thanks to Nathan Garner?

"In case you aren't aware of it, I love you, little brother," she said, not trying to still the quaver in her voice.

A suspicious glitter formed in his dark eyes, quickly followed by a horrified expression, as if he feared he might be in danger of embarrassing himself. Abruptly he pulled away from her and escaped out the door. But she noticed that the typical teenage slouch was gone. Even in his haste to get away, he carried himself with a new sense of pride.

It took her several seconds to rein in her own runaway emotions. Finally she turned and faced Nathan. "Thank you—" she paused to steady her voice "—for giving me back my brother."

His brilliant blue eyes warmed, at odds with a deep longing she glimpsed just below the surface. "I didn't do it," he said quietly. "He did."

"Oh, I think you had more to do with it than you want to take credit for." Suddenly she wondered who'd been around to give him hugs during his self-imposed exile from his family. She slid her hands into her slacks pockets to keep from doing something foolish, like sliding them around him. For some odd reason she was certain he didn't think he deserved sympathy.

"You gave him some very good advice," she said to cover the uncomfortable silence. "Did you learn it from personal experience?"

"Which advice is that?" he asked carefully.

"About hiding emotions." She debated whether to pursue this, then decided there was too much to lose not to. "Seems to me you do the same thing. Of course, you do it for a different reason."

He shifted ever so slightly as if bracing himself. "Meaning?"

"Robert hides his feelings so his friends will think he's tough." She looked at him, her gaze direct. "You, I think, hide yours so no one will guess how much you care."

His eyes became unreadable. "What makes you think that I simply don't care?"

When he'd first returned to Thunder Ridge, she'd wondered if that were the case. But not any longer. He cared and cared deeply. It wasn't that he didn't want others to know; it was himself he was trying to protect from the truth.

"No, I don't think so."

"Ah, Rachel, you're still a romantic," he chided softly, "always searching for qualities that aren't necessarily there."

His mild censure stung, and suddenly she didn't want to risk any more of his disapproval. "Maybe I do."

He simply watched her, and for a brief second a look of profound sadness seemed to darken his features, as if he were carrying unbelievable pain—or guilt. One day soon she intended to discover why he felt he had to hold himself at arms' length. Again his expression became shuttered, and she knew today wasn't the day.

She retrieved her purse, uncertain how much longer she could control the urge to go to him, to wrap her arms around him, to give him the comfort he seemed intent on denying himself. She walked over to the door and opened it, then paused and turned back to him.

"But I've learned that there are some people you can never fool."

Later that night in his father's study, Nathan stared into the deepening darkness, conceding that he wasn't going to be able to hold Rachel's words at bay any longer. For most of the evening he'd managed, with Robert's help, to keep himself too busy to think. He'd attacked the chore of painting the upstairs bedroom as if the fate of the free world depended upon finishing it. Even Robert had made a couple of disparaging comments about his single-minded determination. But he'd gone home over an hour ago, leaving Nathan alone with his thoughts.

Reluctantly he admitted that he'd been fooling himself, hiding from his past, hoping that by doing so he could protect his wounded soul. He fingered the small key still inside the lock of his father's black box where Rachel had left it. She'd found the key. Was he strong enough to face what it unlocked?

He smiled grimly. He'd wanted to find peace—that had been his purpose in coming home. But the only way he was ever going to find peace, he acknowledged, was to come to terms with the past. It was time to get his life in order, time to stop running.

Not giving himself a chance to change his mind, he unlocked the box, took out the envelope and ripped it open. The date, in his father's distinctive script, indicated the letter had been written mere weeks before his death.

Dear Son,

There are so many things that I must tell you and I don't know when or if I will see you again. You are my younger son, but I always considered you far stronger than your brother. Your imposing size and your strength of character made it seem natural to expect you to take care of others. I never realized until recently how unfair that was to you.

By asking you to look after Matthew, I asked the impossible. I fear you mistakenly believe that I blame you for his death. I do not. I could not. For each of us is ultimately responsible for our own actions on this earth.

What we mistook for strength in your brother was in reality naiveté, almost to the point of stubbornness, even recklessness. My dearest wish is that Matthew could have been more like you. Perhaps if he had been, he'd still be alive.

I should have told you this while you were home for his funeral, but in my own grief I failed you. Since then, there has been little communication between us. Truthfully, I never was much good at telling you what was in my heart. Rather than risk these things remaining unsaid, I've written them down. Forgive me for taking so long.

Please know how extraordinarily proud I am of you, and that your mother and I love you.

Dad

Nathan laid the letter gently on the desk, closed his eyes and leaned his head against the back of the chair. Breathing against the tightness in his chest, he tried to sort through all the thoughts and feelings whirling around inside him.

His father had respected his strength. Yet it had been that strength, used unwisely at a critical point, that had resulted in Matthew's death. Would his father have been as forgiving if he'd known? That was something he was destined never to learn. Nathan sighed and pinched the bridge of his nose, feeling years of frustration and loss give way to a sense of acceptance.

He'd been given a precious gift. Questioning it would be pointless. Apparently his father had accepted him for who and what he was, even though he hadn't known how to relate that to a son so different from himself and his firstborn. It explained why Nathan had never known how his father felt about him. Until now. Because of Rachel, he had some hope of finding a measure of peace.

So, why didn't he feel content?

The insistent ring of the phone stopped Rachel as she hurried out the front door. So much for making it to work on time, she thought ruefully. Well, it wouldn't be the first time recently; since her conversation with Nathan at the church six days ago, being late had almost become a habit. Too many restless nights. The image of Nathan's raw expression just before she'd walked out the door kept sneaking back to haunt her. Sighing, she retraced her steps and grabbed the receiver.

"Hello?"

"Rachel? This is Valerie Anderson. I hope I didn't call at a bad time."

Picking up on the distress in Valerie's voice, Rachel took a calming breath and began again. "Of course not, Valerie," she said, instilling the gentler tone she'd learned to use to soothe patients. "What can I do for you?"

A lengthy pause followed, and Rachel thought she heard a low groan.

"Valerie? Is everything all right?"

"I…think—" there was another pause "—I think…I'm in labor."

"Where are you?"

"At…home."

Valerie and Gus lived in one of the old mill cabins on the outskirts of town. Rachel glanced uneasily out the window at the rain. It had been coming down steadily for two days, turning the back roads around the area into a quagmire. "How far apart are your contractions?"

"I'm...not sure. Maybe five...minutes. But I'm not due for another two weeks," Valerie wailed.

"Well, babies have a habit of setting their own schedules." She tried to sound reassuring. "Is Gus there with you?"

"I haven't...seen him since last night." Rachel could hear Valerie's distress begin to escalate into panic. "Is my baby going to be okay?"

"Of course. Everything's going to be fine."

She hoped. She glanced out the window again. She'd made the trip to Valerie's cabin once with Nathan in his van. A steep half-mile stretch of dirt road was the only way in or out. Barely serviceable under the best conditions, it would become impassable except by four-wheel drive or motorcycle during prolonged periods of rain. An ambulance would never make it. Neither would her car.

"Rachel? What...should I do?"

"You shouldn't do anything except stay calm and think about welcoming your baby into the world. I'll be there as soon as I can."

She hung up and dialed Nathan's number, praying he would be home.

As if in answer to her prayer, Nathan picked up on the second ring.

Despite the rain and grisly road conditions, Nathan managed to get Rachel to the small cabin in record time.

Before the van had come to a complete stop, she grabbed her medical bag, opened the door and jumped out. Moments later he followed her up the rickety porch stairs two at a time.

They found Valerie in a back room, curled up on the bed. She was wearing a simple blue robe over a plain nightgown. Her eyes were closed, and she looked pale even against the pristine white sheets. He glanced around the tiny room. Though shabby, it appeared meticulously clean.

"How're you doing?" Rachel asked, easing down beside her on the bed. She picked up one of Valerie's hands and pressed three fingers against the inside of her wrist.

The younger woman's eyes fluttered open, and her mouth curved into a relieved, though exhausted, smile. He'd seen doctors, nurses and various other medical personnel take countless pulses over the years, yet never before had he noticed the elementary procedure convey such compassion, such reassurance. So, what made it different now?

Because this was Rachel.

"Thank you for coming," Valerie whispered.

"Thank Nathan and his trusty four-by-four."

Another contraction bowed her body, and Valerie clutched the covers until her knuckles turned white. Rachel laid her hand gently on the distended tummy, periodically checking her watch until the contraction subsided.

"Looks like your baby's in a hurry to put in an appearance," she teased.

"Do you think…we'll make it…to the hospital?" Valerie asked as she struggled to catch her breath.

Rachel's eyes connected with his long enough for

him to detect a trace of doubt. She returned her attention to her patient. "First we need to find out how things are going, okay?"

Valerie nodded, and Rachel pulled a stethoscope and blood pressure cuff from her bag. She quickly took the readings, then reached for another instrument, this one unfamiliar to him. Fascinated, he watched her use it to listen to the baby through the wall of its mother's stomach. When she finished, Rachel got up from the bed and patted Valerie reassuringly on the arm. Walking over to the door, she motioned for him to follow.

Once outside the door, he moved closer to Rachel to keep their conversation from carrying. "She going to be all right?" he asked.

"So far everything looks good, but she's further along than I'd like." Rachel glanced over her shoulder at Valerie, who seemed to Nathan to be gathering strength for the next onslaught. "I'll know more after I've determined how far she's dilated and checked the baby's position."

He wasn't certain exactly what all that meant, but he was certain he didn't like the worry he read in Rachel's eyes. She seemed too fragile to have to make these decisions, and he wished there was some way he could make it easier for her.

"I'll be right outside." He gestured toward the front of the house. "Call if you need me."

"I'll let you know when I'm done." She sent him a brief smile and went back to tend to Valerie.

Reluctantly he went out onto the broken-down porch, recognizing the need to give them privacy, yet loath to leave Rachel to face this alone. He felt powerless and didn't particularly care for the feeling. Looking around him, he searched for something to take his mind off Rachel and what was going on inside the cabin.

The cabin, he noted, was barely habitable. It hadn't seen fresh paint, inside or out, probably in decades. There were signs of several rotting boards, and he'd noticed dark patches on the ceilings that indicated the old tin roof had begun to leak. From what he could tell, the only things going for the place were running water, electricity and a phone. That an innocent child should be condemned to live in conditions like these never failed to anger him.

Bone-rattling thunder threatened to split the sky open, and lightning sliced the midday gloom as the rain beat out a metallic rhythm on the roof. It seemed like hours before he heard Rachel call him, and he practically bolted the short distance to the bedroom. She didn't look up when he entered.

"It's too late to move her," she said without preamble. "She's too far along. Delivering the baby here will be safer than attempting it in the van on the way to the hospital."

As if giving confirmation, Valerie let out a muffled groan. It was the first sound of distress she'd allowed herself to make since they'd arrived.

"Can you do it here—" he looked around their dismal surroundings "—alone?"

"But I'm not alone." Rachel spared him a swift glance and another smile. "You're here. Are you up to helping?"

An unfamiliar sense of panic rushed at him. Help deliver a baby? He was used to dealing with kids out of their heads on drugs, or running from the law, or half dead from gunshot wounds. He had absolutely no experience bringing a newborn into the world. What if he did something wrong, somehow caused irreparable harm?

But this was Rachel asking him for help. She was willing to trust him, depend on him, even though he'd failed her in the past. He found that kind of faith in him unsettling and prayed it wasn't misplaced.

"Tell me what you want me to do," he finally said.

His consolation was seeing her smile intensify with profound gratitude. She reached up and laid her hand against his cheek, her touch brief, just long enough to create an indefinable bond between them. Then she withdrew her hand.

"Let's do it, then."

She gave him no time to dwell on whether he was or wasn't up to the task. She issued orders, and he followed them as best he could. Over the next several minutes he gathered the supplies Rachel told him she needed, and between the two of them they managed to get a rubber sheet under Valerie seconds before her water broke.

Now Rachel focused totally on her patient and the task at hand. If she was the least bit daunted by what lay ahead, she never let it show. She offered Valerie a soft flow of words meant to soothe, comfort, calm, while containing a subtle note of command. Her cool efficiency amazed him, considering that at the moment he felt anything but cool.

But it was the joy that glittered in her eyes that he found most arousing. The irreverent thought came out of nowhere, and he mentally shook himself. Someone should have informed his unruly libido that her long braid and practical clothing weren't meant to look sexy.

"See if you can support her shoulders," Rachel directed, bringing his mind back to the matter at hand.

He slid his arm under Valerie's straining shoulders and carefully lifted, quelling his feeling of incompetence.

"Come on, honey," Rachel crooned encouragingly. "Push."

The contractions increased in intensity, coming faster and faster, giving Valerie little time to catch her breath before the next one assaulted her body. At some point she'd grabbed hold of his hand in a grip that threatened to crush bones. That she could continue to endure this kind of abuse and still keep going awed and humbled him.

"That's it. Good girl," Rachel exclaimed, praising her efforts. "We're almost there. Give me one more. Now!"

With one final exhausted shriek, Valerie pushed a tiny, thoroughly disgruntled scrap of humanity into the world.

Rachel gently tugged the infant free and turned him over. "You have a son," she said exuberantly.

Quickly she suctioned out the baby's nose and mouth, gave him a cursory exam, then laid him on his mother's stomach while she tied off and cut the umbilical cord. Valerie made a weak attempt to reach for her son, but it was obvious she didn't have the strength. Picking up the squirming infant, Rachel wrapped him in a receiving blanket.

"Here," she said, holding out the baby to Nathan. "Take care of him for a few minutes while I take care of his mommy."

He froze, unsure just how to go about it. The kids he dealt with in his work were usually in their teens. He'd deliberately steered clear of the younger ones. His eyes met hers over the small bundle.

A soft smile lit Rachel's. "Hold out your arms," she instructed gently.

As she settled the tiny infant into his arms, his heart did an odd little flip-flop. He'd helped, if only in a small way, to bring this new life into the world. That something so tiny could be alive seemed a miracle. The baby weighed next to nothing, barely filling his two hands, utterly dependent on the adults around him entrusted with his care. He would need infinite amounts of love, which, Nathan was already finding, would be all too easy to give. Even covered in blood and mucus, he was incredibly beautiful. He walked a few feet away, giving Rachel time to do what was necessary for Valerie, giving himself time to come to terms with the emotions buffeting him.

Before fate or an angry God had changed his life irrevocably, he'd dreamed of having a family with Rachel. A little girl with her compassionate heart. A boy with her unfailing determination. He hadn't allowed himself to think about that dream in years.

What if this were his and Rachel's child? The emotions that exploded inside him almost took his breath away. This was what life was about. This, he realized with blinding certainty, was what he still longed for. The thought shook him to the core.

Valerie made a protesting sound and again reached for her son, apparently beginning to regain some of her strength.

"Give her the baby," Rachel said, smiling. "She deserves a reward for all her hard work."

The amount of reluctance he experienced as he nestled the baby tenderly in its mother's waiting arms unsettled him. Making certain Rachel no longer needed him, he headed back outside. Sometime during the last hour, a thickening fog had replaced the rain. The air was humid, but far less oppressive than what he'd become accustomed to in D.C. He took in several deep lungfuls.

He'd come to believe there was little left that could shake him. One by one, he'd carefully closed off the vulnerable parts of himself. He'd learned to compartmentalize his life. He considered himself a realist. The kids he dealt with were ones on the brink of self-destruction. He tried to save the individual child, never dwelling on the failures, never counting on the successes. It was a bleak life, but it was safe. Now he felt the first cracks in his emotional armor give way, leaving him exposed.

And it terrified him.

Chapter Sixteen

The whine of the approaching motorcycle reached Nathan through the thickening fog a few seconds before it emerged into the clearing that ringed the cabin. No one had to tell him that the rider was Gus Anderson.

Anderson pulled to a stop at the foot of the steps and cut the engine. Glancing up, he registered Nathan's presence on the porch. Not taking his eyes off him, he slowly climbed off the bike.

"What the hell are *you* doing here, preacher man?"

Not a promising opening, Nathan decided and sighed inwardly. Straightening away from a wooden pillar that valiantly worked at supporting the sagging roof, he stood easy, legs braced wide, his weight balanced on the balls of his feet. The stance wasn't threatening, yet it would give him a small advantage should there be trouble.

It had been a long while since he'd been forced into

a fight. His size and his carefully cultivated reputation for being fair-minded usually precluded most challenges from the kids he dealt with in D.C. Gus Anderson, however, was an unknown quantity.

"Doing your job." Nathan's deceptively mild tone would have warned a more prudent man to tread lightly.

But caution seemed lost on Anderson. He bristled and started up the steps. "Meaning?"

"Meaning looking after your sister."

"Valerie?" He took the last three steps in one bound. "Where is she?"

Nathan nodded toward the house. "Inside."

Anderson's gaze darted to the doorway, then back to him. "What's going on? What's wrong with her?" he demanded, a poorly concealed dread slipping past the belligerence.

"Where was your concern last night," Nathan challenged softly, "while your sister was alone and about to go into labor?"

"Labor?" Anderson visibly paled and started across the porch.

Nathan caught his arm before he could reach the door. "Not so fast," he said, keeping his tone neutral but his grip firm. "Rachel Holcomb is with her now. Give her a chance to finish up."

He yanked unsuccessfully against Nathan's hold. "I warned that woman to stay away from my sister. If anything happens to Valerie," he growled, "I'll kill her."

Nathan's gut knotted with apprehension—a feeling that always preceded a situation about to go sour. He recalled how poorly last week's confrontation with Gus Anderson had ended. Nothing had been settled, and instinct had told him then that at some point Anderson would retaliate. And that next time would require a whole lot more than arm wrestling.

Even so, he'd foolishly harbored the faint hope that there might be a chance to salvage the younger man, that he might come to his senses. Instead, his hostility seemed to have turned him into an unpredictable threat. Nathan hoped he hadn't made a crucial mistake by deciding against putting a decisive end to the problem when he'd had the opportunity.

Rachel suddenly appeared in the doorway. In one sweep her gaze took in both men, then dropped to his hand still gripping Anderson's arm. Alarm briefly flickered across her features, before she composed herself.

"Will you two please keep it down?" she said, as if confronting two men on the trigger-edge of a brawl were an everyday occurrence. "You're upsetting Valerie and scaring the baby."

"Baby?" The news seemed to stun Anderson. "Val's not supposed to have the baby for a couple more weeks."

"Yes, well, what can I say? Babies are notorious for doing things their way. In any case, your sister just delivered your nephew, and what she needs right now is peace and quiet." Without waiting to see whether her suggestion would be heeded, she turned to Nathan. "We should get them to the hospital immediately."

"Hospital?" Anderson parroted for the third time.

Reluctantly Nathan released Anderson's arm and moved toward the steps. "I'll get the van."

"Hurry," Rachel told him. "Bring it as close to the steps as you can. Valerie's too weak to walk. We'll have to carry her."

Anderson stepped closer to Rachel. "What's wrong

with my sister?'' he demanded. ''What have you done to her?''

The fear beginning to edge Anderson's words made Nathan glance back. When he saw Rachel reach out placatingly to Anderson, he hesitated.

''She'll be fine once we get her to the hospital. I'll explain on the way. Okay?'' she said to Anderson. ''Right now we should get moving.''

Nathan understood she was trying to convey the need for haste without arousing undue alarm. But instinct told him she hadn't succeeded. He read the panic in Anderson's eyes a split second before Anderson seized her and slammed her against the cabin's rough siding. ''I warned you to stay away from my sister!''

Rational thought fled, leaving Nathan with the primal urge to protect Rachel. Praying he wouldn't make matters worse, he lunged, wrenching at the harsh fingers biting into her shoulders. ''Back off, Anderson,'' he growled.

''Please, Nathan.'' She appeared remarkably calm, considering her precarious situation. ''Let me handle this.''

Leave it to Rachel, he thought grimly, to believe she could handle something like this on her own. The woman was totally oblivious to danger. It would be almost comical—if it wasn't so terrifying. This was the third time he'd witnessed her pull a similar stunt. And he'd discovered repetition didn't make it any less frightening. God alone knew how many other instances there had been, or might be in the future. He didn't want to hazard a guess. He didn't think he could handle the answer.

''I don't think that's such a wise idea,'' he suggested next to her ear. Fear for her safety mixed with fury at himself for not having anticipated this scenario. He pried at the unyielding hands gripping her shoulders, but Anderson simply dug his fingers in harder, causing Rachel to wince.

She might believe herself invincible, but she couldn't withstand a mauling by someone the size of this bastard. A red haze blurred Nathan's vision. He knew without doubt that by tomorrow there would be bruises on her delicate skin.

"Gus, listen to me," she said, disregarding his advice as expected. "This isn't doing Valerie or the baby any good." She keep her tone reasonable. "They both need help that I can't give them. They need to be in the hospital."

Anderson shoved his face close to Rachel's, one hand pressed menacingly against the base of her throat. "Then you shoulda let somebody who knows what the hell they're doing take care of her," he snarled, giving her a rough shake. "I told you she needed a *real* doctor."

With screaming certainty Nathan realized that reasoning with Anderson was useless. He was on the thin edge of completely losing control. How much more volatile would he become now that he'd convinced himself that Rachel had caused his sister harm?

A replay of what happened to Matthew six years ago burst with blinding clarity into his mind. He'd hesitated then, and his brother had died. He wouldn't repeat that mistake.

Without pulling his punch, Nathan sent his fist slamming into Anderson's kidney. Anderson gave a muffled grunt, his grip loosening a fraction. It was all Nathan needed to free Rachel and shove her to safety.

Recovering quickly, Anderson charged Nathan, driving a shoulder into his midsection, ripping the air from his lungs in a painful whoosh. Both men thudded against the scarred floor of the porch. Nathan fought for breath, and Anderson used the opportunity to smash a fist into his jaw with bone-jarring accuracy. His head snapped back, and his mouth filled with the metallic taste of blood.

Momentarily stunned, he shook his head to clear it and braced for the next blow. Over the clamor of scuffling bodies, he could hear the high-pitched wail of the baby and Valerie's distressed calls coming from inside the cabin. In his peripheral vision he caught sight of Rachel still frozen to the spot where he'd shoved her out of harm's way, a look of horror on her face.

Damn. He had to put an end to this. Now. Time had come to rethink his strategy. Somehow he managed to stagger to his feet and haul Anderson up with him. Relegating the consequences to the back of his mind and giving Anderson no time to get his bearings, Nathan delivered a well-placed knee to the groin, followed by a solid uppercut to the chin.

Anderson went down for the count.

Not the most laudable method of handling the situation, Nathan conceded wearily as he wiped blood from his mouth with the back of one hand. But it got the job done. When dealing with aggressive punks, he'd learned a long time ago that sometimes the only option was to use the most expedient means available.

Several hours later Nathan paced the small waiting room, barely conscious of his myriad aches and pains. His dominant thought was discovering for himself just how badly today's events had affected Rachel. She'd given him repeated assurances on the drive from the cabin to the hospital that she was fine. But she'd been distracted by her two patients—and, he was certain, by the memory of the violence she'd just witnessed—and her assurances hadn't quite convinced him.

Once they arrived, she'd disappeared inside with Valerie and the baby. Over Nathan's strenuous objections, the admissions nurse, a woman who'd obviously had extensive training as a drill sergeant, had insisted that he be checked over by a doctor. With scant patience he'd tolerated the probing, the X-raying and the patching up, his only consolation being that Anderson was suffering the same fate. Now, he simply wanted to talk to Rachel.

Hearing footsteps in the corridor, he glanced up to see Gus Anderson enter the room and come to a halt in front of him. A purpling eye and swollen jaw made it difficult for Nathan to judge Anderson's exact frame of mind. So he braced himself, feeling his abused body protest painfully.

"I've been looking for you," Anderson said.

"Looks like you found me," he observed laconically.

The memory of how this punk had attacked Rachel generated a fresh surge of anger. Keeping himself in check wasn't going to be one of the easier things he'd ever done. In the years since he'd left Thunder Ridge, envisioning Rachel safe and happy had given him a small measure of comfort. It might have been a fantasy, but he'd never allowed the idea of possible harm coming to her to mar it. Seeing Anderson manhandle her today had irrevocably destroyed it. For that, Nathan doubly resented him.

He'd learned to face street fights, drug overdoses and all the other misery connected with inner-city life. What he couldn't face, he finally admitted, was the possibility of losing Rachel. Now or ever. Rather than finding that thought disturbing, Nathan felt a sense of peace settle in a part of him that had been restless for too long.

Anderson shifted uneasily. "I—" he began haltingly "—owe you an apology."

It took a moment for Anderson's words to get past his own distracting thoughts. When they eventually sank in, they surprised him. But while he recognized what saying that must have cost Anderson, he wasn't quite ready to relent.

"No, you owe Rachel. And your sister. But somehow I don't imagine apologizing to a woman for attacking her will be easy—even for you."

Anderson's eyes narrowed. "Anything's easy, if the reason's good enough. Look, man," he said defiantly. "I was trying to protect my sister."

"Protect her from what? Certainly not Rachel. She was there to help. If it hadn't been for her, your sister would've had to deliver her baby by herself."

A look came and went on Anderson's features that might have been called remorse. "Yeah, I know. But I kinda lost it when Rachel said Val and the baby had to get to the hospital in a big hurry." He shoved his fingers through his short-cropped hair. "Guess I, uh, figured if something was wrong with them, she was to blame."

"In other words you *kinda* jumped to the wrong conclusion," Nathan said, hanging on to his anger by a thread. "You couldn't wait long enough to find out that your nephew might need to be in an incubator because he was born early. Or that giving birth at home might be harder on your sister than if she'd been in the hospital."

Hunching his shoulders, Anderson scowled but didn't argue. "I guess. Look, I didn't mean to hurt Rachel."

"Tell *her*," Nathan said tersely, "not me."

"I plan to," Anderson snarled back.

Despite himself, Nathan felt the stirring of grudging respect. Anderson had owned up to what he'd done. He'd apologized. He hadn't tried to defend himself. He'd even tolerated being berated reasonably well.

"Maybe if you'd lose the attitude," Nathan suggested mildly, his anger beginning to recede, yet not quite ready to let Anderson off the hook, "you'd be less likely to make a similar mistake in the future."

"Yeah, maybe," Anderson said noncommittally but without rancor. He began prowling the room, finally coming to stand again in front of Nathan. "I still owe you an apology."

"How do you figure that?"

Anderson eyed him. "You took a beating, too."

Critically surveying Anderson's cuts and bruises, Nathan experienced the briefest twinge of conscience. There was no doubt Anderson had been in a fight. This wasn't how a minister was supposed to deal with problems. And he knew without doubt that this wasn't how his father or brother had ever dealt with them. In fact, Matthew had died trying to prove that violence was never the answer.

"Oh, I don't know," he said, after a moment. "I'd say we're about even on that score."

A sheepish grin started across Anderson's face to be cut short by a pained grimace. "Maybe."

Nathan gingerly fingered his own aching jaw and grimaced himself. "Guess we should both be thankful there're no broken bones."

This time Anderson did manage a grin and nodded in agreement. Then he grew serious again. "I…uh…"

He searched for the right words. "Thanks for taking care of Val and...the kid."

For the second time today Anderson had surprised him. "It's Rachel who deserves your gratitude."

"Yeah, I know. Fact is, she's the only person in this town who's ever shown any interest in Val."

"Can't imagine why that could be," he commented, his tone sardonic.

Anderson seemed to silently debate with himself for several moments before continuing. "When Val found out she was pregnant and the bum had skipped out on her," he began haltingly, as if uncomfortable discussing personal matters, "I wanted to get her outta the 'hood, find a place to start over. Someplace she could have a decent life, her and the kid."

That Anderson had been concerned enough for his sister to go to these lengths to help her confirmed Nathan's belief that he couldn't be all bad. "What made you choose Thunder Ridge?" Nathan asked.

He shrugged. "I figured the people in a small town would, y'know, be friendly."

"Well, if you're looking for friendship, you sure picked a peculiar way of finding it."

Anderson sent him a questioning look. "What d'you mean?"

"Intimidating the town's residents, beating up kids and roughing up women," he suggested gently, "isn't going to endear you—or anyone else in your family, for that matter—to many folks."

The young man looked momentarily stricken, as if that idea had never occurred to him. Nathan was beginning to understand. He could relate to Anderson's concern for his family. It was important to Anderson that they be accepted into the community. Problem was, he apparently didn't have a clue how to go about it.

"Ever think of treating people the way you want to be treated? Proving to folks that you *deserve* to be accepted?"

A movement in the doorway interrupted them. Nathan turned his head to see Rachel, arms crossed protectively around her waist, hovering just outside the room. Wondering how long she'd been standing there, Nathan scanned her pale features and troubled eyes. In the space of a heartbeat, two thoughts flashed through his mind. The first was the fact that, though fatigue had painted dark smudges under her eyes, she appeared to be physically okay.

The second was that he loved this woman beyond life.

She looked from one man to the other. "I hope," she commented a little too brightly, "this doesn't mean one of you is going to start throwing punches again."

He knew he had only himself to blame for that trace of apprehension. A deep sense of regret that she'd been drawn into the altercation between Anderson and himself settled like a rock in his chest. He wanted to go to her, cradle her against him, tell her everything was okay. Then he wanted to strip her naked and determine for himself the extent of her injuries.

No, he silently corrected, that didn't begin to describe what he wanted. Nor what he intended to do.

For now he opted to keep things light. "Not me," he said, carefully wiggling his jaw back and forth. "I've had my quota for a while. Might not be so lucky next time."

She studied him, her eyes still troubled. "I doubt luck has much to do with it."

Gus started edging toward the door Rachel had just entered. "Uh, thanks for taking care of my sister…and the kid," he mumbled to her, his face flushing a dull red. "Sorry if I—" he gestured awkwardly "—y'know, hurt you or anything. Uh, I better go check on Val."

Rachel watched Gus's rapid departure from the room. "Wow, I'm stunned. A thank-you and an apology all in one breath." She brought her gaze back to Nathan and found him studying her with a disturbing intensity. She cleared her throat and pasted on a smile. "I didn't realize Gus Anderson possessed a socially acceptable side. You must be into working miracles."

"No miracles. Just gave him a couple of suggestions to chew on."

"Let's hope the taste continues to have such a soothing effect." She finally had to glance away from his potent study.

"How's Valerie?" he asked.

"She'll be fine. We got the hemorrhaging under control, and she's resting comfortably."

"And the baby?"

She sent him a small satisfied smile. "The pediatrician said he came through like a trooper."

"And you?" He thrust his hands into his pockets, looked down at his boots. "How are you holding up?"

Automatically she kneaded her left shoulder and winced. "A long, hot soak, something to eat and about twelve uninterrupted hours of sleep—preferably simultaneously," she said longingly, "and I might survive."

Checking her watch, she silently groaned. Only a few minutes past eight. With Robert waiting at home, it would be hours before she'd be able to indulge herself.

"If that's what it takes to revive you," Nathan said, sauntering over to her. "I know just the place."

He was much too close and she felt much too vulnerable. Suppressing the urge to take a step back, she quipped, "Paradise?"

"Even better." He slipped an arm around her shoulders.

She surprised herself by allowing him to guide her through the door of the waiting room and down the hall. "What could be better than paradise?"

"Home." He appeared momentarily startled by his own answer.

"I thought that's where I was going anyway."

He suddenly smiled down at her, a smile filled with some unreadable promise. "Not yours. Mine."

She felt the familiar rush of excitement. Dangerous. He'd captured her with that same smile, she remembered wistfully, from the first day they met. "I don't seem to have any say in the matter," she muttered to herself.

"Nope," he agreed, as if she'd meant her comment for him.

She didn't bother to correct his mistake, instead allowing herself for the present to be swept along by his compelling magnetism.

"We'll figure out what to feed you when we get there," he continued, directing her through the automatic doors guarding the hospital entrance. "I'll fix it while you soak as long as you like. When you're finished eating, I'll tuck you into bed in your old room."

Her stomach did an odd little flutter at his last suggestion. It sounded so tempting. She was bone tired and ached in places she hadn't even identified yet. Right now her defenses were nonexistent. And self-preservation told her the very last thing she should expose herself to was Nathan Garner fussing over her.

They strolled in the direction of the parking lot. Signs of the recent rain had vanished, she noticed, leaving a brilliant canopy of stars poking holes in the night sky. The pleasantly warm air smelled freshly scrubbed clean and held only a hint of the hot humid summer to come. She took in a deep breath, hoping it would clear her head.

"While the offer sounds lovely, I'll have to settle for a gallon of strong coffee. Robert will be waiting for me," she reminded him.

He slowly shook his head. "Already been taken care of. Ran into Paul McDaniel earlier. He said he'd make sure Robert got fed and had someplace to bunk in for the night." In the yellowish glow of the security lights, he continued to watch her with those intense blue eyes. "Any more excuses?" he asked quietly.

Why was she fighting it? she wondered. She'd determined weeks ago that she wanted to discover what deep secret he guarded with such painstaking care. Here was her chance.

Tonight had confirmed one fact that she'd only suspected until now: Nathan Garner had a gift for working with troubled youth. Though he might not want to acknowledge it, that was what he was meant to do. And she knew, even though it was painful to admit it, that eventually he would return to that world. A hollow ache filled her heart.

She loved this man. She wanted to spend what little time was left with him—no matter what price her heart would ultimately have to pay.

"No," she finally said, allowing him to help her into the van. "No more excuses."

Chapter Seventeen

Even after the water had grown lukewarm, it took the aroma of something mouthwatering to make Rachel leave the old ceramic tub. Stepping out, she was amazed to discover she felt rejuvenated, her earlier fatigue gone. She wrapped herself in the huge white towel Nathan had left out for her and sighed blissfully. An uninterrupted bath was a luxury she didn't often get. With a teenager in the house and only one bathroom, she'd learned that sticking to showers—and *quick* ones, at that—kept hassles to a minimum.

Giving herself a critical look in the mirror over the pedestal sink, she realized the steam had caused her hair to begin slipping from its French braid. With quick, efficient movements, she tucked the damp strands into a new one. Her stomach rumbled hungrily, reminding her that it had been hours since she'd last fed it. Now if she could find something to wear, preferably something more comfortable than what she'd had on for the past fourteen hours, she'd track down whatever smelled so delicious and greedily devour it.

Glancing around the spacious master bath to locate the closet, she noted how lovingly Nathan had redone it. Fresh paint, new wallpaper, not a chipped tile in sight. With a sinking feeling she realized that he'd almost finished fixing up the house to put it on the market.

Immeasurable longing welled up inside her. She didn't want someone else to enjoy his meticulous hard work. In a carefully guarded corner of her heart, she allowed herself a brief, foolish dream. This should be Nathan's home. And hers. She exhaled an irritated puff of air and reminded herself again how painful wishing for impossible things could be.

Straightening her shoulders, she went to the closet, opened the door and pulled out a navy blue terry-cloth robe that had to belong to Nathan. She hesitated, then decided she didn't care whether he minded her borrowing it or not. Slipping it on, she was immediately enveloped by his unique scent. As she followed the delicious smells to the kitchen, she wasn't certain which was more tempting. The scent of food. Or the scent of Nathan.

She found him standing in front of the stove, ladling steaming potato soup into two bowls. He looked over at her as she walked through the kitchen door and halted his task. His gaze traced a slow path from her freshly braided hair to her bare feet, then returned to settle on her eyes. Before she could put a name to the emotion in his, he masked his response with one of his high-voltage smiles.

''I don't believe I've seen you this relaxed since I've

been home,'' he said casually and turned back to the stove.

"That makes us even, then," she said, "because I don't remember the last time I've felt this relaxed." She snagged a potato chip and munched. "Can I help?"

"Everything's ready. Just grab that plate of sandwiches and take it over to the table." He followed, carrying the bowls of steaming soup. He set one in front of her and took the seat across from her.

"I'm starved," she said, tucking into her soup. After several sinful spoonfuls, she added, "Heavenly. One of my favorites. Thanks for fixing it."

"You're welcome."

"Which reminds me. I haven't gotten around to thanking you for everything else you did today."

"No problem," he drawled. "Glad I was here to help."

"You were more help than you know. I don't mind telling you I was just a wee bit rattled when things began to get hectic."

His blue eyes warmed with what might have been admiration and approval. "No one would have guessed."

"What can I say? Knowing how to put on a good act is absolutely necessary in my line of work. Can't have a mother in labor thinking her midwife is scared out of her mind."

His smile expanded into a chuckle.

She sank her teeth into a thick sandwich of spiced beef, closed her eyes and savored it. After swallowing, she said, "Anyway, thanks. I thought we made a terrific team."

He stopped eating to watch her steadily for several heartbeats. "We always did work well together."

His comment generated an ache deep within her. She wanted badly to ask, *Then why did you leave?* She reined in the impulse. "I also wanted to tell you, that despite my initial reservations, I was impressed with how you handled Gus."

A startled expression crossed his face, quickly replaced by a grimace. "The way I see it, if I have to resort to violence, there's not much to shout about."

She frowned slightly. "Well, I'll agree that witnessing a fight isn't on my all-time favorites list. And I can imagine being in one must be even less appealing. But in this case you weren't given much choice."

Shaking his head, he said, "I should've been able to prevent it."

"Are you always this hard on yourself?"

He looked at her for a long moment. "When it involves violence, yes."

She was beginning to get an inkling that he was hard on himself about a lot of things. For several minutes they both concentrated on their food. Finally she broke the silence. "Does it happen often?"

Nathan polished off the last bite of his sandwich. "What?"

"Having to resort to violence."

He chewed thoughtfully for several moments. "It depends. When you're dealing with a kid on the edge of self-destruction, you have to get him to listen to some hard truths. Since most of these kids believe anything an adult has to say is garbage at best or an outright lie at worst, you have to prove that what you say is the exception. That requires getting his attention—which usually means acting as tough as he *thinks* he is."

"Like challenging him to arm wrestle."

The smile that tugged at his mouth was wry. "That's

one of the more benign methods. Then you pray you can convince him that violence isn't the answer. That at some point down the line, he won't be the toughest, baddest dude on the block. Then he stands a good chance of dying.'' He stood abruptly and began clearing the table.

How heartbreakingly frustrating that must be, she thought, for someone like Nathan. Hurting for him, she wondered how many kids he'd been unable to convince. She wasn't certain she wanted to find out.

He fixed them both a mug of hot tea and brought it back to the table, then sat down again. ''So, to answer your question,'' he continued, ''I don't have to resort to strong-arm tactics all that often, but it's more often than I'd like.''

In sympathy she laid a hand on his arm and felt the muscles bunch under her fingers. ''I overheard some of what you said to Gus at the hospital tonight. You must know you have a gift for working with these kids.''

He picked up his mug, cradling it in his hands, a troubled look darkening his eyes. ''I wish that were true.''

''You've certainly helped Robert,'' she reminded him.

''Like I told you, Robert's basically a good kid.''

She picked up her own mug. ''And Gus? Which column does he fall in?''

Nathan exhaled a heavy breath and shook his head. ''Who knows? One sure thing I've learned is nothing's a sure thing. We made a good start today, but…'' He let the thought trail away and shrugged.

''No, *you* made a good start.''

The beginnings of a smile played at his mouth. ''You win some, you lose some,'' he said, sounding almost philosophical. "But those victories, that's what make the battle worth it."

She sipped her tea thoughtfully and wondered if he was aware of the underlying satisfaction evident in that statement. From what he'd left unsaid, she gathered he must have experienced situations far more traumatic than she could imagine. And they had marked him profoundly. But some instinct told her that no matter how painful, his work was a vital part of him. That the two could not be successfully separated. That realization made her heart constrict painfully.

He took a swallow of tea. "Do you have any idea how many times I've drunk this particular blend of tea," he said, "and thought of you?"

His comment was so unexpected that it took her a moment to collect herself. "That's interesting. I was sure you forgot I existed years ago," she said, allowing just a touch of sarcasm to slip in.

His intense gaze moved over her face until she felt as though he might read her thoughts. "My first night back in town, I told you I'd never forgotten you."

"Then how could you have stayed away?" she blurted out, and immediately regretted her wayward tongue.

He sighed and set down his mug.

"Sorry." She held up her hand. "Don't answer that. I don't have any right to ask."

"Yes, you do," he said. "It should have been discussed long before now." He scrubbed his hand over his face. "I didn't come back because I couldn't. It's as simple and as complicated as that."

It took her a moment to absorb the fact that he seemed to be opening the conversation to a discussion of the past. ''Are you going to explain?'' she asked, testing her theory.

''Matthew died because of me.''

The stark statement stunned her. She sat absolutely still and listened as he began telling her about the day his brother was killed. It was obvious he'd seldom spoken of it. He remained dry-eyed as he spoke, but profound agony resonated in his rough voice, in the hoarse words.

A small group of rebel soldiers had come to the small missionary outpost, waving guns and threatening the locals. ''They'd been drinking,'' Nathan continued. ''But Matthew was certain he could convince them to leave before they harmed anyone. My gut told me he was dead wrong.''

Nathan left his chair and began pacing the kitchen. ''I tried to get him to back off, but Matthew wouldn't listen, kept insisting he could handle it.'' He shook his head. ''He always took too many chances.''

''What did you do?'' She held her breath, one part of her wondering if he'd continue, another almost wishing he wouldn't.

His laugh held no humor. ''Not a damned thing. He ordered me to stay out of it. He was senior man and he was in charge. So I ignored every one of the warnings screaming in my head. I knew—''

He wandered over to the window and stared out into the darkness, as if it offered an escape from the demon pursuing him. ''I *knew* preaching wasn't going to work. The only thing those guys understood—the only thing they respected—was physical force. Our only hope was to convince them that we were prepared to fight if the situation demanded it. But Matthew wanted no part of that.'' Nathan rolled his shoulders. ''Then it was too late.''

He didn't have to tell her the rest. She recalled clearly hearing some of the people who attended Matthew's funeral whispering about the gory details.

''I should've listened to my gut.'' He shook his head. ''I was supposed to look after him. I failed.''

''But it's not your fault,'' she said with absolute conviction even as she struggled with the fact that he hadn't bothered to discuss something this life-altering with her. ''Everyone knew how stubborn Matthew could be. He made the choice, not you.''

As he talked about his brother's death, she'd sensed that though it still caused him enormous pain, he'd come to terms with it. And that he'd done it without her.

Raw pain, pain she thought she'd put to rest long ago, rolled through her on a vicious wave. Nathan hadn't trusted her enough to share a major part of his life with her. The man who'd said he loved her, asked her to marry him, had chosen instead to exclude her from it.

''And it never occurred to you that you should tell me this?''

''I'm telling you now,'' he said simply.

She inhaled sharply. ''Well, you're about six years too late.'' He was being brutally honest; she would do no less. ''When you left immediately after Matthew's funeral without an explanation,'' she said around a hitch in her throat, ''at first I was confused and incredibly hurt. But I kept telling myself eventually you'd come home. When you didn't, I just plain got angry.''

He turned to face her, watching her with those clear, unreadable eyes. ''I don't blame you,'' he said. ''I broke my promise to you.''

She shook her head emphatically, feeling rekindled anger begin to burn away the pain. "That doesn't begin to explain why I'm angry."

"No? Are you saying you *didn't* want me to come home?"

"Of course I did," she said. "But I could have lived with your decision not to...*if* you'd bothered to discuss your reasons with me."

Nathan frowned. "You want to explain that a little more?"

"You told me you loved me. You asked me to marry you." The need to be on an equal footing with him compelled her to stand up. "I expected you to *talk* to me, tell me what was going on, what you were feeling. You should have told me you believed leaving Thunder Ridge was best for you. I might not have liked it, but I would have understood." She struggled to rein in her emotions. "Instead you ran," she said. "And you kept running."

"You're right," he said, offering no argument. "I was a coward."

His frank admission dampened her anger. Taking a deep breath, she composed herself. She was long past hurling accusations or throwing temper tantrums. Now she simply wanted to learn as much as he was willing to tell her.

"Why D.C.?" she asked after a moment. "What did it offer that you couldn't find here?"

"A place where no one knew me," he said simply.

She studied him in confusion. "Didn't you find that a bit lonely?"

"Yes, but it comes with anonymity. And that's what I wanted."

Which confirmed that he hadn't needed her. "You've

lost me," she said, struggling to understand. "It seems you'd have been better off near the people you loved, who loved you, who could help you face your ghosts."

"Someone who's guilty of letting his brother be murdered isn't entitled to that kind of comfort," he said. "And to be completely honest, I didn't want to face the people I'd failed. You wouldn't have liked me very much during that time, Rachel. I wasn't a very nice person."

She'd never seen Nathan like this—brutally honest, holding nothing back, painting himself in the most unflattering light. A few weeks ago he'd been reluctant to talk about himself or the past; now he couldn't seem to tell her enough. It was almost as if he were testing her.

"You're wrong, you know," she told him quietly. "I've seen you in more than one situation where it was so hard for you to be good." She smiled whimsically. "But you always managed to do it anyway. That's one of the things I loved best about you."

"You always saw me as some sort of magician who could make everything right. I couldn't make it right for my brother."

"I've never expected you to do anything," she told him levelly, "but be what you are. Why are you telling me this?"

Something flared in his eyes. "They say confession's good for the soul." He slid his hands into the back pockets of his jeans. "And I wanted you to know who I am, *what* I am, warts and all."

"I've always known who you were, Nathan. It's you who didn't seem to understand yourself."

"I hope you mean that."

"What made you decide to tell me this now?"

Despite the puzzling shadow of insecurity she

glimpsed in his eyes, he walked toward her with slow, purposeful strides. When he reached her, he pulled his hands out of his pockets and lifted them to cradle her face. He searched her eyes, and the intensity of it almost forced her to look away.

"Because," he said very gently, "I badly want to make love to you."

Chapter Eighteen

Rachel's anger drained away, drowned out by the enormity of his words. *This time Nathan had asked.* Her heart tripped over itself. Doubtful her legs would continue to support her, she brought her arms up to circle his neck and leaned into him.

"It took you long enough," she told him evenly.

Heat blazed in his eyes, turning them a brilliant blue. "Don't tempt me, Rachel," he warned, "unless you mean it. Tonight's not a good time for games."

She felt an answering heat, and it gave her courage. He'd said something similar weeks ago when they'd stopped at the river to talk. But that had been to warn her away. Tonight was different—she'd make certain of that.

"No?" She smiled up at him provocatively. "Why?"

"Because I don't have the strength to deny you—"

Nathan sucked in a harsh breath when she lifted her mouth up to his "—or myself."

He kissed her. He poured everything into it—the need, the desperation, the years of deprivation—and prayed his hunger wouldn't frighten her away.

Yet she didn't act frightened. In fact, she met him eagerly move for move.

Rational thought faded, leaving one fundamental driving need: to mate with this woman, make her a part of him, make himself a part of her. He'd waited an eternity for this. A distant inner voice reminded him that if he didn't get a handle on the consuming need clawing at him, their first time together would be on the kitchen floor. It took superhuman effort, but he managed to lift his mouth from hers.

Rachel moaned in protest and reached for him.

"Wait." He battled for control. "I want to do this right. Let's go upstairs."

Her mouth looked bruised, wet from his; her eyes unfocused, softened with arousal. Her gaze made a languid circle around the room. When it finally returned to his, he caught a mischievous sparkle. "Are you sure you want to?"

"No," he said wryly, "but we're going anyway."

He scooped her up and carried her to the master bedroom. Once there, he slowly lowered her to her feet beside the bed. He found it more than a little unsettling to discover that the interruption had done nothing to cool his blood.

He reached for the belt holding her robe closed, unsurprised to see his hand tremble. It would be a miracle, he thought wryly, if any part of him functioned properly. "I think you're wearing my robe," he said, hoping to ease some of the tension.

She cocked her head and smiled. "Do you want it back?"

"You can't begin to imagine how much." He tugged at the belt, and the robe fell partially open. Reverently he reached out to trace one exquisite lace-covered breast.

And she trembled.

His heart pounded inside his chest. He wanted her with a hunger that challenged every principle he'd tried to live his life by. But more than anything else, he wanted this to be right for her. He swallowed, and his hand dropped away from her breast.

"I'm not sure everything's in working order. It's been a long time for me."

"Well, that makes you at least one up on me."

His body went absolutely still. The ramifications of what she was suggesting staggered him. "Never?"

Gazing unflinchingly up at him, her eyes softened to velvet. "Never," she confirmed.

Primitive satisfaction warred with sudden indecision as conflicting emotions played havoc with what little was left of his self-control. "Why?" he asked helplessly.

"The right situation never presented itself after you left."

She'd waited for him? Did he have a right to do this now? he wondered. *Should* he? "Maybe this isn't a good idea," he said, struggling to contain the need still raging through him.

Something flickered in her eyes, then was gone, replaced by a bold smile. "Let me remind you, Nathan Garner, that this time it was your idea that we make love. If you think I'm going to let you back out now, think again."

This time. Her teasing statement held a wealth of longing—and betrayal. "You're sure?"

"Absolutely," she said with certainty. "I figure I better grab you while I can. Besides," she added softly, "there's no one else I'd rather have initiate me."

"Rachel." He closed his eyes, inhaled sharply. "You take my breath away." He covered her mouth with his, barely managing to keep the kiss tender. Then he raised his head.

"The hardest thing I've ever done," he said hoarsely, "was leave you." Although he was beginning to realize that this time would be infinitely harder.

"Then stay with me now." It was a simple statement and hit him with the force of its sincerity.

"Ah, Rachel." He framed her face with his hands. "I couldn't leave if my life depended on it."

From some inner source he hadn't known existed, he summoned the control necessary to proceed slowly. He eased the robe off her shoulders to fall in a dark heap on the floor, then allowed his gaze to roam over her. Blood pounded through him. She'd been sunbathing recently, he thought absently. The pale pink bra and panties contrasted sensually with her lightly tanned skin.

His gaze returned to her face, and he found her watching him, her eyes reflecting a hint of self-doubt. "Do I get to do the same?"

He would have laughed aloud if he hadn't been in such agony. "Sweetheart, you can do anything you want."

Her eyes warmed sexily, and somehow he found the willpower to stand perfectly still while she went to work on the buttons of his shirt. What seemed an eon later, she pushed it off him, dropped it to the floor and ran her hands over his chest. When her mouth followed her hands, he wasn't certain how long he could remain standing. She left a trail of mind-destroying kisses down his chest, across his stomach to the waistband of his jeans until she was kneeling in front of him.

She hesitated and looked up at him. "You can't imagine how often I've dreamed of this." She smiled shyly. "But ridiculous as it may seem, I'm not sure what to do next."

Feeling his self-control teeter on the thin edge of oblivion, he gave a harsh groan and pulled her to her feet. "Then let me show you."

Arousal made him clumsy, yet somehow he managed to shuck out of his jeans and, with less finesse than he'd have liked, get her out of her bra and panties. Then slowly he drew her to him until her naked body rested against his. The initial contact stole his breath.

"I want this to be right for you."

"If it's with you, it will be," she said with such trust that he felt shaken to the core.

Lifting her, he laid her on the bed and came down beside her. She immediately turned to him.

"Open your eyes, Rachel," he gently commanded. "Look at me."

She lazily focused on his face and sent him the sweetest, sexiest smile. With infinite care he slid into her welcoming body until they were joined as closely as humanly possible. Everything in him was attuned to how *right* this felt. Even as he filled her, she filled a void that had been inside him for as long as he could remember.

His gaze burned into hers. *I love you, Rachel,* he told her silently, pledging his heart, his mind and his body. *I will always love you.*

But he didn't allow himself to utter the words. This time, he wouldn't make her any promises. This time he would *prove* to her that she could trust him.

Her eyes fluttered closed. The beginning of her sensual contractions triggered his own release, and as the last of his control abandoned him, he gave himself up to the need pouring through him.

With his last coherent thought he realized that for the first time in as long as he could remember, he felt whole, complete. She'd given him back a part of himself he'd thought forever dead. He prayed he could do a fraction as much for her.

Minutes or maybe hours later, Rachel slowly became conscious of Nathan's warm body resting against her back. His even breathing close to her ear told her he was asleep. It would be no trouble at all, she thought longingly, to get used to the feel of him cradling her like this through the night. Easing out of his hold, she propped on one elbow to study him.

Except for the determined set of his jaw, he appeared relaxed…almost content. Her heart swelled with love. She allowed her gaze to wander over the darkly tanned skin covering the firm muscles of his chest, before traveling lower still. For so many years she'd yearned for the right to be this intimate with Nathan. Now having experienced the soul-shattering act of making love with him, she wondered how she'd survive giving him up.

And she would have to. Nathan's leaving was inevitable.

She recalled with aching clarity that he'd carefully avoided speaking of the future, had made no promises. Had not said he loved her.

Her heart contracted, even though the logical side of

her understood that their situation was impossible. She couldn't go with him. Moving Robert to the inner city, especially at this critical stage of his young life, was out of the question. Nor could Nathan stay here—not when she knew without doubt that his life was in D.C., working with troubled kids.

Over the past several weeks she'd become aware of the fact that people thought nothing of asking Nathan for help. Including herself. Yet no one seemed to ask him what he needed. But she knew. Whether he was ready to accept it or not, his work was an inseparable part of him. He needed it as much as it needed him.

The simple truth was that she loved him too much to see him forced to choose between her and his ministry.

He'd already given her so much; she could at least give him that. Somehow she'd find the strength not to beg him to take her with him, or beg him to marry her as she'd done years ago. She wouldn't ask him to stay. She'd accept his lovemaking and whatever time they had left together as the precious gifts they were. And though it would rip her heart out, she wouldn't ask for more.

She suddenly looked up to find him awake, his probing eyes watching her. Feeling self-conscious at being caught openly examining him, she said the first thing that popped into her head. ''You sure don't look like a minister.''

He chuckled, a deep, intimate sound that heated her blood. ''You can bet this is one time I'm very glad of it.''

Folding her arms across her chest, she rested her chin on her forearms. ''I had no idea a minister could be such a wonderful lover.''

Embarrassment darkened his cheeks. ''I'd say that's

debatable." He touched a finger to her mouth. It was tender from his kisses and the stubble of his beard. "I was too rough. Are you all right?"

Drawing his finger into her mouth, she gave it a playful nip. "I've never been better," she assured him.

Something flared in his eyes. "You've given me back my soul."

"Hush," she said, covering his mouth with her hand and smiling down at him. "You shouldn't say that."

"Ah, but I have to," he said around her fingers. "It's a sin to tell a lie."

Outwardly he might be teasing, but she detected an underlying sober note. Best to change the subject, she silently prompted, before she ended up breaking her newly sworn promise.

She glanced around the master bedroom. The walls had been recently painted a fresh white and the trim a soothing taupe. The oak floor had been redone until it gleamed with a warm patina. It was an inviting room, one she could imagine spending long hours of pleasure in.

"You've done a wonderful job with this room," she said, hearing the longing in her voice. "In fact, with the whole house."

His intense gaze bored into her for several heartbeats, then seemed to relent. "Thanks. There're still a few things I have to do, even more I'd like to do."

"Like what?" However foolish, she wanted to hear his plans. It helped prolong the fantasy of one day sharing a life with him here.

He folded an arm behind his head, but kept the other anchoring her firmly to his side. "I'd like to see this place like it was when I was growing up. Remember? With horses and chickens and a big garden."

She chuckled reminiscently. "How could I forget? I spent too many hours weeding the garden or running from the chickens or begging to ride the horses."

Her eyes came back to his face. Time to instill some logic into this conversation, she decided, before her wayward heart led her too far into that fantasy. "But of course, you couldn't put that kind of work into this place, not when you're going to sell it."

Some quickly concealed emotion shadowed his eyes as he watched her intently. "Maybe."

She steadied her breathing. "We both know you have to go back."

"Do we?" He shrugged and sighed heavily. "Unfortunately, you're right. I do have other duties to take care of."

Even though she'd prepared herself, his casual acquiescence sliced deeply into a vital part of her. Time for a reality check. If she wanted to make the most of their remaining time together, she couldn't brood about things that could never be.

She ran her hand provocatively down his chest. When he sucked in a harsh breath, she smiled.

"Then we shouldn't waste any more time."

Rachel glanced up from the task of gently packing dirt around the base of a fuchsia begonia plant to see a dark green pickup turn into the driveway. It came to a stop a few feet from where she knelt in one of the flower beds in the front yard. Pushing to her feet, she shaded her eyes against the bright July sun and watched Nathan get out and slowly walk toward her.

She hadn't seen him since their one night together over two weeks ago. She'd heard, courtesy of the town gossips, that he'd been busy putting the finishing touches on his house. Her gaze hungrily surveyed faded jeans hugging narrow hips, then traveled up to a white T-shirt molding a chest she knew from intimate exploration was rock solid. Her stomach gave an erotic flutter. A slight breeze caught at his hair, and she noticed with a pang of longing that the relentless Georgia sun had finally bleached it to the honey color she remembered so well.

Part of her wanted to run to him, throw her arms around him and try to recapture what they'd had that night. A saner part prevailed, and she stood her ground. He looked leaner, and as he drew closer she could see dark circles under his eyes. Was it because he'd been having as much trouble sleeping as she? Or was it because he'd been driving himself to get the job done so he could get back to his real life? Either way, something told her this wasn't just an ordinary visit.

She pasted on what she hoped was a believable smile. "What brings you here? We haven't seen you in a while."

"I've been busy. Finally finished the house."

"Then it's ready to go on the market?"

"It's ready." He studied her intently. "How are you, Rachel?"

Keep it light, a small voice prompted. She smiled brightly. "Couldn't be better."

His smile only turned up one corner of his mouth. "That's good to hear." He shoved his hands into his pockets. "And Robert?"

"He's fine," she said. "Staying out of trouble, now that the gang activity around the area seems to be under control."

One by one, the reasons for Nathan to remain in Thunder Ridge had disappeared. However foolish, she'd nourished a tiny hope that by some miracle *she* might become a reason to stay.

He nodded and glanced around the yard. "I wondered if you had any objections to Robert keeping the motor-cycle?"

Her gaze shifted to the truck, noted the bike anchored to the bed, then moved back to him. A sense of inevitability pressed in on her. "You mean permanently?"

"Yes," he said. "I don't have a need for it any longer."

A cold fist squeezed her chest. She knew what the bike had represented to Nathan: impermanence, mobility, freedom. Now he was offering to give it away. His redemption was complete. He no longer needed an easy means of escape. Yet she knew, even without his saying it, that he was leaving Thunder Ridge—this time to go back to his life in D.C. An impossible sorrow that it wouldn't include her closed in on her. She intensified her smile, determined Nathan wouldn't guess her feelings.

"Well," she said, opting for a humorous touch, "if I said no, something tells me my life would suddenly become a waking nightmare. So that pretty much narrows down the answer. Besides, I think Robert might be ready to handle the responsibility now. Lately he's begun to act a lot more mature. He's inside. Shall I call him?"

"Please," was all he said.

She ran lightly up the porch steps. "Robert?" she called through the screen door. "There's someone here to see you."

Her brother clattered down the stairs and out onto the porch. "What's up?" he asked.

"I understand you just got your driver's license," Nathan said.

Robert grinned. "Yeah, last week."

Nathan nodded toward the truck. "Thought you might be interested in taking the Harley off my hands."

Robert's delight didn't quite disguise his confusion. "You mean it?"

"I wouldn't say it if I didn't."

He loped to the back of the truck and looked longingly at the bike, then turned to Nathan. "How come?"

"I figure if you have your own bike, you won't have a reason to get mixed up with another biker gang."

Robert sobered. "I don't hang with them anymore." His smile returned. "But I'll still take the bike."

Nathan grinned. "Then let's get 'er off the truck." Together they unfastened the cables holding the motorcycle in place and rolled it down the ramp.

When it was on the ground, Robert looked at Nathan. "Why would you wanna give it away?"

"I've got to head back to D.C. And I wanted her to have a good home."

So it was true, Rachel thought. This time the hand squeezing her heart almost took her breath away.

"D.C.?" Robert frowned. "If you're leaving, who's going to help me work on it?"

"Oh, I imagine someone will turn up." He placed his hand on Robert's shoulder. "I have unfinished business waiting for me there," he explained. "People I care for, people who need me, depend on me."

He spoke to Robert, but Rachel felt his gaze burn into her. It was as if his words were meant for her. He'd finally accepted the fact that he couldn't give up his work.

"That sucks," Robert said succinctly.

Rachel didn't bother to correct him. Her brother's comment represented her sentiments exactly. "Why don't you take the motorcycle for a spin?" she said to Robert.

Obviously startled by the suggestion, he asked carefully, "You don't mind?"

"Hey, don't push it," she warned good-naturedly. "The best I can say for now is that I'll tolerate it. Stay right in this area, though. And be home by supper."

He grinned. "Thanks, Rach." He picked up the helmet and tucked it under his arm, then walked over to Nathan and held out his right hand. "Thanks, man," Robert said. "I'll take good care of it."

Nathan clasped Robert's hand and shook it. "You're welcome," he said. "One more thing…"

"Yeah?"

"Look after your sister."

Robert's eyes narrowed, and his gaze moved from Nathan to her then back again. "All right," he said slowly. "You got it."

Rachel's heart constricted. Her brother had grown up. She watched him walk to the bike and climb on. "Be careful," she called after him as he roared down the driveway.

When Robert and the bike had disappeared over the hill, and the noise had dwindled away, Nathan returned his gaze to her. "This time I wanted to make sure I told you I was leaving."

Rachel wasn't certain she would survive the pain. Every atom of her being wanted to beg him not to do this. But she'd sworn she wouldn't.

"Thank you." She squared her shoulders. "It's best that you go."

"Is it?" He continued to watch her steadily.

"You know it is," she said in resignation. "You couldn't walk away from your work with those kids, any more than you could stop being a minister." She knew she was reinforcing with words what she'd already decided. "If you tried, you might as well stop breathing."

"Thank you for understanding."

He stepped closer, and she went willingly into his arms, eager for this final physical contact with him. At first his mouth settled tenderly over hers, before the sharp edge of desperation turned it greedy. The kiss seemed to hold both farewell and promise—a promise he gave her no opportunity to decipher. She felt him shudder, then he took her by the shoulders and gently, resolutely set her away from him. Without another word, he strode to the truck, got in and drove away.

Rachel felt what was left of her heart crumble inside her chest.

Chapter Nineteen

Rachel shifted in the church pew, waiting for Sunday services to begin. The infamous August heat and humidity pressed in on her, and she wondered what had possessed her to wear the white linen suit rather than a sensible sleeveless dress. But a restless feminine need for a change, to make a statement to the world, had convinced her to choose the suit.

She'd been brooding since Nathan's departure six weeks ago. It was time to get on with her life. And she'd decided that today was the day to begin. Out of the corner of her eye she caught Robert's concerned gaze on her and turned her head to smile at him in reassurance.

He smiled back, handsome in his shirt and tie, and she felt a jumble of pride and sadness. He'd gone from a rebellious adolescent to a maturing young man in a few short months. Thanks to Nathan. Quickly she put the brakes on that line of thought. She had to stop thinking about him. He was the past; for her own salvation, she had to think of the future.

After the choir and congregation finished singing the opening hymns, Reverend McDaniel came to the pulpit. Because he was known for keeping his sermons brief and to the point, she, like most members of the church, looked forward to hearing him speak.

But after only a few chosen words, he said, "I'm not going to deliver my usual sermon this morning. Instead there's someone here who wants to say a few words." He beckoned toward the door off to one side of the sanctuary and smiled. "I'll turn it over to you now," he said to the figure standing in the shadows.

Amid a buzz of speculation, everyone in the church craned their heads to get a glimpse of the unexpected guest. As the man emerged from the side room, Rachel felt her heart stop midbeat before kicking into overdrive.

Nathan Garner.

What was he doing back in Thunder Ridge? She'd been certain she'd seen the last of him. But here he was, striding up the aisle, every bit as irresistible as she'd tried to convince herself he wasn't. It took a moment for the reality to sink in. Why hadn't she heard at least a hint of a rumor? Where was the gossip mill, she wondered ruefully, when you really needed it?

Determinedly she refused to speculate about what might have brought him back. He was simply passing through, she told herself firmly. Nor would she dwell on why he hadn't bothered to contact her; it would only lead to more heartache. She snorted in disgust. Hadn't she spent the better part of the past six weeks putting all the "what ifs" to rest?

The most startling thing about him was that he was wearing a suit. Suits had never been Nathan Garner's style. She could recall him having worn one on only a handful of occasions. But today he looked confident, relaxed. And purposeful. As he came abreast of her, their eyes connected, and her breath lodged in her throat.

Nathan Garner was a man at peace with himself.

Nathan resisted the urge to tug at his tie. He couldn't remember the last time he'd worn a conventional suit. Certainly not in the ghettoes of the nation's capitol. There, the punks would have considered it nerdish, taken it as a sign of weakness. At the very least he would have been laughed out of the area; at worst, beaten to a pulp and left for dead in some dark alley. But here a suit was expected, and he wanted nothing to detract from what he was about to say.

Reaching the steps to the pulpit, he felt his belly muscles knot in apprehension. He paused long enough to glance up at the stained glass window that overlooked the sanctuary. *Help me do this right.*

He mounted the steps, feeling decidedly out of his element. He hadn't been in a pulpit since shortly after seminary school. He might be a minister, but he'd never been a preacher, always a doer. But preaching wasn't his purpose here today.

''Good morning.'' His eyes sought out Rachel, sitting off to his right, three rows from the front, absolutely motionless. He gripped the sides of the pulpit, aware that everyone in the room was focused on him, including her.

''Most of you know me,'' he continued. ''For those of you who don't, I grew up here in Thunder Ridge. It was in this town that I made the decision to become a minister.''

Rachel noticed that everyone around her had leaned forward, waiting to hear his next words. She did the same as curiosity slowly replaced her initial shock at seeing Nathan back in town.

''But I wasn't a very good one,'' he added matter-of-factly. ''When things got a little rough, I ran, tossed aside everything that was important in my life, including someone who meant more to me than life itself.''

Murmurs of disapproval began to ripple through the congregation. Robert reached over and squeezed her hand. Suddenly she began to wonder if she was ready to find out where this was leading.

''It took me a long time, but I finally learned that nothing worthwhile comes without a price, and usually an extremely high one.''

There were nods of understanding and agreement, and Rachel found herself holding her breath.

''What I'm getting around to is this. If you're agreeable, I'd be honored to be your minister.''

With a grinning Paul McDaniel leading the group, the congregation broke into enthusiastic applause.

Nathan raised a hand to quiet them. ''I can't say that I'm worthy, but I can promise to give you my best shot. And I give you my solemn word I won't turn my back on you again.''

Her heart ached. For years, she'd yearned to hear those words. When they finally sank in, she was on her feet. ''Wait a minute. What about your work in D.C.? You can't give that up.''

His gaze connected with hers, and she felt the jolt to the depths of her soul. Then his eyes warmed, and he raised a questioning eyebrow. ''I can't?''

The congregation avidly followed this new development, directing their attention from first one to the other.

"Of course not," she said. "It's too important to you."

"You're right, as always, Rachel," he said gently, then scanned the congregation. "Which brings me to what I'd like to discuss with you next."

Suddenly remembering where she was, she sat down. All eyes again focused on him.

"I plan to convert my home here into a modified working ranch again, with a big garden, some chickens, a few horses."

Everyone waited expectantly.

"That's what I *plan* to do. What I'd like to do, with your permission, is to bring disadvantaged inner-city kids there for short visits. That way they can learn another life-style, get away from the danger and violence that's so commonplace in their lives."

His gaze came back to her. "You see, Rachel? I'll still be working with the kids."

She nodded. She heard his enthusiasm as he carefully detailed his plans for bringing in kids. He was deeply committed to this new plan. A part of her rejoiced while another ached. None of it would include her.

A few people in the congregation murmured their concern, and Nathan raised his hand.

"I know, I know," he continued. "This is asking a lot of you folks. But we've proved this community can handle problems if we work together. And this is something that I believe is important."

The murmurs subsided until one church member stood and said, "Well if you're gonna be in charge of it, we figure it'll work out okay." He looked around at the others. "Right?"

One by one they began to add their agreement.

"Thank you," Nathan said humbly. "Your confidence means a great deal to me." Nathan's gaze settled on her. "There's one other person whose confidence I hope to gain today."

Rachel's breath froze in her lungs as she experienced a dawning hope that she futilely tried to suppress.

"It's because of Rachel Holcomb that I found my way back home. Although she doesn't believe it, she's my salvation. She gave me something precious, her trust and her belief in me, at a time when I didn't believe in myself."

The ice that had encased her heart since Nathan left six weeks ago began to thaw.

"She told me I had to go back to D.C. And she was right. But not for the reasons she thought. I had to go back to tie up loose ends."

As he continued to speak, tears slipped slowly down her cheeks. Robert put a protective arm around her shoulders, hugging her fiercely.

"Well now I'm back, as I should have come back six years ago. With all my ghosts buried and with something worthwhile to offer now." He started down the steps of the pulpit and walked over to her. "I love you, Rachel Holcomb."

The church members sitting around her moved out of his way. Robert gave her a squeeze and moved with them. But Nathan stopped at the end of the pew, and her heart began to pound.

"What I want to know is," he said hoarsely, almost pleadingly, "are you going to make an honest man of me?"

There was a collective gasp that erupted into loud cheers. But everything around her began to fade into the background. She looked into Nathan's crystal blue eyes, shocked by the gut-level fear she saw there.

She was out of her seat and in his arms in a flash. "Yes!" she said, loud enough for everyone to hear. "Yes, yes—"

He cut off her words with his mouth. The kiss contained all the despair and heartache of the past six weeks, but it also contained a promise—a promise of forever.

When he finally raised his head, they realized that they were alone in the sanctuary. "It took you long enough," she said teasingly.

"This time I had to do it right." He kissed her again. Hard. "I want to hear you say it."

"I love you, Reverend Nathan Garner." He kissed her again. Harder. "Does this mean you're going to perform the ceremony?"

"Not on your life. I want to concentrate on you, watch you promise yourself and your love to me for eternity."

And they sealed the pledge with a kiss.

* * * * *

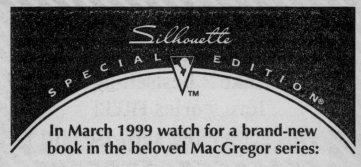

If you enjoyed what you just read,
then we've got an offer you can't resist!

Take 2 bestselling
love stories FREE!

Plus get a FREE surprise gift!

Clip this page and mail it to Silhouette Reader Service™

IN U.S.A.
3010 Walden Ave.
P.O. Box 1867
Buffalo, N.Y. 14240-1867

IN CANADA
P.O. Box 609
Fort Erie, Ontario
L2A 5X3

YES! Please send me 2 free Silhouette Special Edition® novels and my free surprise gift. Then send me 6 brand-new novels every month, which I will receive months before they're available in stores. In the U.S.A., bill me at the bargain price of $3.57 plus 25¢ delivery per book and applicable sales tax, if any*. In Canada, bill me at the bargain price of $3.96 plus 25¢ delivery per book and applicable taxes**. That's the complete price and a savings of over 10% off the cover prices—what a great deal! I understand that accepting the 2 free books and gift places me under no obligation ever to buy any books. I can always return a shipment and cancel at any time. Even if I never buy another book from Silhouette, the 2 free books and gift are mine to keep forever. So why not take us up on our invitation. You'll be glad you did!

235 SEN CNFD
335 SEN CNFE

Name	(PLEASE PRINT)	
Address	Apt.#	
City	State/Prov.	Zip/Postal Code

* Terms and prices subject to change without notice. Sales tax applicable in N.Y.
** Canadian residents will be charged applicable provincial taxes and GST.
   All orders subject to approval. Offer limited to one per household.
   ® are registered trademarks of Harlequin Enterprises Limited.

SPED99   ©1998 Harlequin Enterprises Limited

And Baby Makes Three
FIRST TRIMESTER
by
SHERRYL WOODS

Three ornery Adams men are about to be roped into fatherhood...and they don't suspect a thing!

And Baby Makes Three

APRIL 1999
The phenomenal series
from Sherryl Woods has readers
clamoring for more! And in this special collection,
we discover the stories that started it all....

Luke, Jordan and Cody are tough ranchers set in
their bachelor ways until three beautiful women
beguile them into forsaking their single lives for
instant families. Will each be a match made in
heaven...or the delivery room?

Available at your favorite retail outlet.

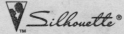

Silhouette

SPECIAL EDITION®

™

That's My Baby!

**Don't miss these poignant stories coming to
THAT'S MY BABY!—only from
Silhouette Special Edition!**

December 1998 THEIR CHILD
by Penny Richards (SE# 1213)
Drew McShane married Kim Campion to give her baby
a name. Could their daughter unite them in love?

February 1999 BABY, OUR BABY!
by Patricia Thayer (SE# 1225)
Her baby girl would always remind Ali Pierce of her
night of love with Jake Hawkins. Now he was back—
and proposing marriage!

April 1999 A FATHER FOR HER BABY
by Celeste Hamilton (SE #1237)
When Jarrett McMullen located his long-lost runaway
bride, could he convince the amnesiac, expectant
mother-to-be he wanted her for always?

THAT'S MY BABY!
*Sometimes bringing up baby can bring surprises...
and showers of love.*

Available at your favorite retail outlet.

™ *Silhouette* ®

COMING NEXT MONTH

#1237 A FATHER FOR HER BABY—Celeste Hamilton
That's My Baby!
When Jarrett McMullen saw Ashley Grant again, the sweet beauty he'd
once loved and let go was pregnant—and alone. And though the amnesiac
mother-to-be couldn't remember her past, Jarrett was determined to claim
a place in her future—as the father of her child....

#1238 WRANGLER—Myrna Temte
Hearts of Wyoming
Horse wrangler Lori Jones knew she'd better steer clear of Sunshine Gap's
ruggedly appealing deputy sheriff, Zack McBride, who was close to
discovering her darkest secret. But then the sexy lawman took her boy
under his wing—and made a lasting impression on Lori's wary heart!

#1239 BUCHANAN'S BRIDE—Pamela Toth
Buckles & Broncos
He was lost and alone…but not for long. As luck would have it, feisty
cowgirl Leah Randall rescued the stranded stranger, tenderly took him in
and gave him all her love. But would their blossoming romance survive
the revelation that this dynamic man was a long-lost relation of her sworn
enemy?

#1240 FINALLY HIS BRIDE—Christine Flynn
The Whitaker Brides
After nearly a decade, Trevor Whitaker still left Erin Gray breathless.
Their bittersweet reunion brought back memories of unfulfilled passion—
and broken promises. But her ardor for this devastatingly handsome man
was intoxicating. Would Erin's fantasy of being a Whitaker bride finally
come true?

#1241 A WEDDING FOR MAGGIE—Allison Leigh
Men of the Double-C Ranch
When Daniel Clay returned to the Double-C ranch, the tormented cowboy
knew he was unworthy of his beloved Maggie. But when their night of
love left Maggie pregnant, Daniel stubbornly insisted on a convenient
union. But then a headstrong Maggie made a marriage demand of her
own....

#1242 NOT JUST ANOTHER COWBOY—Carol Finch
Alexa Tipton had her fill of charming rodeo men. So the serious-minded
single mom was beside herself when she became irresistibly attracted to
the fun-loving Chance Butler. The sexy superstar cowboy began to melt
her steely resistance, but could she trust their happiness would last?